Stripmalling

Published by ECW Press, 2120 Queen Street East, Suite 200,
Toronto, Ontario, Canada M4E 1E2
416.694.3348 / info@ecwpress.com

LIBRARY AND ARCHIVES CANADA CATALOGUING IN PUBLICATION

Fiorentino, Jon Paul
Stripmalling / Jon Paul Fiorentino ; Evan Munday, illustrator.

"A misFit book".
ISBN 978-1-55022-859-5

I. Munday, Evan II. Title.

PS8561.I585S87 2009   C813'.6   C2008-907554-4

Editor for the press: Michael Holmes
Type and cover design: Rachel Ironstone
Author photo: Marisa Grizenko
Printing: Transcontinental

This book is set in Minion.

The publication of *Stripmalling* has been generously supported by
the Canada Council for the Arts, which last year invested $20.1 million in
writing and publishing throughout Canada, by the Ontario Arts Council, by the Government of Ontario through Ontario Book Publishing Tax Credit, by the OMDC Book Fund,
an initiative of the Ontario Media Development Corporation, and by the Government of
Canada through the Book Publishing Industry Development Program (BPIDP).

ECW PRESS
ecwpress.com

Stripmalling

A NOVEL BY JON PAUL FIORENTINO
with illustrations by evan munday

MISFIT

ECW PRESS
A MISFIT BOOK

This book is for Robert Allen,
In Memoriam.

The only way to be reconciled to old friends
is to part with them for good.

— WILLIAM HAZLITT,

ON THE PLEASURE OF HATING

Johnny Carson, Shag Carpet, and Polyester

My first memory is of Johnny Carson, shag carpet, and polyester. It is of my grandfather and the smell of whisky and tobacco. It is of the chattering voices of my mom, dad, and grandmother echoing from the kitchen of my grand-parents' apartment. It is now, through the necessary unreliability of memory, about my grandfather's character, and his hopes and his failures. He was a writer of respectable success, in southern Italy.

He wrote in his dialect, Calabrese, and in "proper" Italian. He wrote lighthearted poetry — light verse. He loved to laugh and to make others laugh. He was what you might call a "B-level" writer. Not a famous writer, but recognizable in his time. When he moved to Transcona from Amato, he left his modest fame, became a labourer at the CN Rail shops, and supported a family of seven on his wages. He always wore a suit to work. He never gave up his identity as a gentleman and a writer. I often look at his books and think of the hopes and failures we share. When I realized I could write, I promised myself that I would never let anything get in the way of the work. It was a stupid promise. But I have kept it anyway.

My grandfather and I are in the living room. The wooden-framed television lights the space. The shag carpet is mustard

yellow. My grandfather is in his favourite chair: a green vel-
vet rocking chair. He is wearing a white muscle shirt and
checkered blue and grey polyester dress pants. His matching
blazer is in a heap beside the chair.

My grandfather has a strong cackle and it's frequent
tonight. When he really gets going, he drowns out the laugh-
ter and conversation from behind the wall, in the kitchen.
He is responding to the man on the television — a white-
haired man sitting behind a desk, interviewing various
people, cracking jokes. Johnny Carson. Every time the studio
audience laughs, my grandfather laughs. He doesn't under-
stand English particularly well. But he understands laughter.

I am stuck in between my grandfather's pant legs. I feel
the rough polyester against my skin. At once strangely
comforting and frustrating. I try to crawl away and he lets
me go momentarily. And then he pulls me back toward him
with his legs. I am fixated on the white-haired man on the
television. I want to get closer to him. But I never make it
halfway across the shag. Whenever my grandfather pulls me
closer, I whine a little. This elicits a different kind of laugh-
ter from him. A soft, high-pitched laughter. I like that he
laughs at me. It feels like polyester.

Interruption: Confession

I am getting to a point in my life where I fear absolutely nothing, absolutely no one. It's not that I'm stronger, it's that I'm more comfortable with my weakness. I guess that's a kind of strength. The only things I really fear these days are panic attacks and puppies. Puppies are always looking at me with their soulless eyes, sizing me up, judging me, fucking with my life force.

I would like to write a book that makes the reader feel like a better person but I seem destined to write the kind of books that make people feel ripped-off and embarrassed. I don't know what it is about the stories I write. Why do I dwell on the formative years, the narratives of failure and shame, the dry humping and the huffing? Why don't I just give the people what they want and write about gardens and tea with Aunt Gertrude? And why do I sign book contracts without reading them?

I have tried to write dead "serious" prose fiction, but in the midst of a gripping story like the one about a young, deaf, autistic woman discovering her gift for turkey calling, I always find myself making fun of the earnestness, the characters and most important, myself. In the end I prefer to place my own preciousness where it belongs: in my record-setting Care Bear collection.

Maybe I am a truly fearful person. I know I still fear

not being taken seriously. But how does one get over such a fear? What does getting over a fear mean anyways? Fear is writer fuel. Without fear writers would be lawyers or astronauts or something successful and soulless like that.

So, one day, after doing a great deal of crystal meth, I said to myself: "Jonny, why don't you write an experimental novel of some sort? I mean, you've already vacuumed the living room seventeen times and it's not getting any tidier." And then I vacuumed. And then I set off to write some clean prose. This novel is about a failed writer named Jonny, his mid-life crisis, and his latest failed manuscript, a novel called *Stripmalling*. It's a novel about the little miracles that accompany failure. It's a novel in many voices — all of them mine: the character Jonny, the writer Jonny, and the miserable real-life Jonny. But please note that, as usual, all three Jonnies are fictional. The real Jonny can be found on Lavalife under the tag, sweaty4u2009.

Context: Transcona

A town with strip malls. Old-time strip malls. The kind where your moms and dads own the shops. A town with all-night huffing parties and decrepit community clubs. A town with an Orthodox church, United church, Non-denominational church.

A town with one public golf course. A town with trains. Too many trains. And not enough jobs. A town affectionately known as Trashcona. A town with the most successful son working as a teacher or a civil servant. A town with the most successful daughter waiting till sixteen to get pregnant for the first time.

A town with corrupt cops. A town with inept administrators. A town with toxins seeping into your skin. A town to forget or mythologize in order to remember strategically. A town of fragments. Sentence fragments.

It's Easy to Be a Moralist When You're Ugly

"Say something lovely," I said.

"God, you are such an emotional wimp!" Dora said.

"That's not lovely at all!"

I would always start our telephone conversations by demanding a compliment or a lovely locution. I'm not sure where I got the guts. I would call Dora, night manager of Libby's Discount Fabrics, at the beginning and end of my shift, and during the break. We had started our affair one night when she came by the Shill Gas Station where I worked to trade some bills for coins and we made eyes at each other. She wasn't particularly seductive — in fact, she had an extremely off-putting lazy eye — but her intentions were clear, and I was always up for romance. That's why I stayed at the Regent Park Strip Mall for so long. It wasn't like I didn't have better offers for employment. Hell, my uncle could have scored me a position as a night watchman for a window company in South Transcona if I wanted it. They had a union and everything. But nothing compared to the rich social tapestry of the strip mall. These were my people. This was my home. When I was too drunk on peach schnapps and gas fumes, I would sleep in my little grey Chevette in the middle of the strip mall parking lot and everything would seem right with the world, except for my brain, which was damaged on account of all the huffing.

Dora was a slim young woman in her mid-twenties. She didn't believe in monogamy. She believed that sex was simply fucking and should not be regulated by archaic notions of patriarchal possession. She was taking some courses at the University of Winnipeg. Her ideas intrigued me. Especially the parts about fucking. I called her Dora the Explorer.

When I was a young man all I ever wanted was to have sex with a girl. My mother told me that if I ever had sex, she would know because she knew the smell of sex intimately, and if she ever smelled it on me, she would make me a eunuch. Mom was very concerned for my well-being.

"I have a nose like a bloodhound," she would say. "If any little harpy is going to devirginize my Jonny, she had better be a Christian, it had better be ten years from now, and she had better have a ring. And if any man even thinks about touching my little lamb, I will destroy him. The only man who will ever be inside Jonny is Jesus Christ."

Even though she was my best girl, Dora was not allowed to meet my parents. This was a good policy because she had a tendency to spew gender theory straight out of first-year undergraduate courses. Stuff like: "I am not queer but I am queer-bodied; monogamy is a repellant social construct; we are all hermaphrodites, and the closer we get to our inner hermaphrodicity, the happier we will be." I always found that kind of talk very arousing, but my parents were more apt to find it Satanic. She had a bumper sticker on her Plymouth K-car that said, "Polyamory is not a crime."

"Say something lovely," I said again.

"Okay, I want you to taste Darren's cock."

"Who's Darren?"

"Mmmnngh," she moaned into the phone, "he's this new attendant at Sudsy's Car Wash. You should see him, Jonny. He's very built, super hot, and he seems really freaky too. He's not like you at all!"

"Thanks, Dora."

"Well, let's face it, you're not exactly George Clooney." She always used that line, no matter what the situation. If I was having trouble deciding what to order at a restaurant, she would say, "Let's face it, you're not exactly George Clooney."

I was willing to do anything for Dora. And the weird thing is, I don't think I was actually all that attracted to her. She looked like a world-weary Thora Birch. And she was only in her mid-twenties. I wasn't quite sure of her exact age because I didn't really care about such things. (I was only twenty-one.) But I did care about pleasing Dora. She introduced me to a world in which mutual masturbation and foot licking were not deviant behaviours. When people tried to chastise her regarding her libertinism, she would stare at them and say, "It's easy to be a moralist when you're ugly." She was so fearless, so in control.

I should explain that my mother had not only threatened to lop off my manhood, she was also my Grade 7 sexual education teacher. Transcona was a small town and the educational options were limited. My mom doubled as guidance counsellor and sex-ed instructor at Arthur Day Junior High. I had no choice but to take the class. And my mother had no choice but to teach the class. It was a provincial requirement of our Manitoba NDP government.

I would sit in the back corner of the class as she explained the functions of ovaries and fallopian tubes. And every once in a while she would glare at me as if to say, "You had better not be learning any of this, you little pervert. I'm going to pray those demons of lust right out of you as soon as we get home!" So we made a deal. Mom told me she would give me a solid B in the class if I would just sit there, not pay attention, and do my homework for other classes instead. While the other students got to read pamphlets with titles like *A Boy's Guide to Masturbation* and *So, You're Ready to Be Penetrated,* my mom would supplement my learning with tracts like *Celibacy: The Long Road Ahead.*

Dora had made the arrangements for my very first threesome: it would comprise me, Darren, Dora the Explorer, many candles, and the music of Percy Sledge. I would have much preferred if there were to be two women and me, but I was not in a position to bargain. I would never have been able to experiment if it weren't for Dora's initiative and legwork. I arrived at Dora's bachelor apartment a half-hour early, hoping to express my appreciation and trepidation to her, but Darren was already there and they were snorting coke off the coffee table and making out. I feebly shuffled over to the couch and did my best to join in, but they seemed pretty focused on each other. It was hard to find a way in that wasn't awkward. Darren was hypermuscular, had tattoos all over his hairless arms, and both of his nipples were pierced. He had long, flowing, curly brown locks and the face of a cherub. I suddenly felt like the kid at the pool, too ashamed to take his shirt off, choosing to swim in it and let it cling to his rolls of fat instead. Of course, this was quite a natural feeling since I was always that kid. I stopped rubbing Dora's back, backed away and did a line.

That's when it happened. Darren and I made eye contact. "Hey, champ," he said, and gave Dora a gentle shove to the side. For the next eternity or so, Darren gave me a thorough sexual education. I glimpsed Dora pouting about all the attention I was receiving, but it was pointless to be diplomatic about it. The boy was only interested in me, and frankly, that was a good feeling. For the rest of the night, Dora explored her newfound sense of rejection, I explored a tandem feeling of guilt and arousal, and Darren simply explored me. Eventually Dora asked us to leave, and Darren held my hand and walked me back to my Chevette.

He was a perfect gentleman.

In the end I realized I was not really built for threesomes, or open sexual encounters, or anything involving me taking off my pants. At the time it felt amazing to be desired, but the guilt crept up on me and it was so stifling. In fact, my favourite moments from that time involve lying down with Dora in the back of the Chevette, talking about our hopes and dreams, or queer theory, or whatever. I liked those quiet times, when Dora and I would smoke hash out of the car lighter, and the buzz was nice and mild, and the strip mall was quiet and still, and the mosquitoes danced under the amber floodlights. I guess I'm a bit of a traditionalist. I'm like my mother that way.

Instructions for Asking a Girl to Go Steady

I walked into A Taste of China and waved at Robbie Lyons, the hyper-Scottish proprietor of the restaurant. He smiled an almost toothless smile. Mr. Lyons was a peculiar man who believed in his heart that he was not Scottish, but in fact Chinese, and had therefore become the first Scottish owner of a Chinese restaurant in Winnipeg. He was a heavy-set man with fire-red hair that matched his red and gold Taste of China polo shirt. His menu choices were sometimes strange, like his haggis stir-fry, but he did make a mean General Tao tofu.

"Hey, listen Mr. Lyons, I need to ask you a favour."

"Aye, go ahead, Jonny."

"Can I have a fortune cookie?"

"You want a fortune cookie before you eat your General Tao tofu?"

"Well, I can't stay. I just need to borrow one fortune cookie for a special project."

"Now how are you supposed to borrow a fortune cookie? How will you pay me back?"

"Well, you know what I mean. Can you just give me one?"

"I can't do it, Jonny. I just can't!"

"What? Why not?"

"It's just not right. It goes against the Chinese restaurant code."

"What the hell are you talking about?"

"The Chinese restaurant code. It states that the fortune cookie is not to be taken lightly. Now what do you mean to be doing with this fortune cookie anyway, lad?"

I was getting angry. Real angry. Remember when Jesus went to that bake sale at the temple, and they didn't have any of those chocolate cupcakes he loved so much, and he got really pissed and drove the bake sale participants from the temple with his whip? Angry like that. "Fuck! There's no such thing as a Chinese restaurant code. And even if there were, you're not even Chinese anyway! You're a crazy Scot who thinks he's Chinese."

Mr. Lyons hissed at me. "My God, laddy! Are you daft? I'm Chinese through and through! And I will not tolerate your language or accusations. I made a life choice fifteen years ago. The choice was between being a Scot and being a Chinaman. I chose the world of the Chinaman. Case closed. Now do I have to get Benny to throw you out of here?"

Mr. Lyons started wheezing. He was honestly hurt by the situation and I started to feel quite sorry for him. I wanted to tell him that being Chinese is not a choice. I wanted to explain to him that in fact, if he were Chinese, he wouldn't use terms like "Aye," "Laddy," and "Chinaman." But I just sighed.

"No. I'm sorry, Mr. Lyons. I'll take one order of General Tao tofu to go. But don't forget my fortune cookie, okay?"

"Aye, Jonny. But remember: don't take the fortune for

granted. It's a sacred trust between the Chinese and those fortunate enough to enjoy our cuisine."

"Yes, Mr. Lyons."

When my takeout arrived, I quickly left the restaurant, grabbed the fortune cookie, and dumped the tofu. I had a little art project to do.

For this project you will need the following:

One fortune cookie (in wrapper).
One set of tweezers.
One pair of scissors.
One sheet of blank paper.
A fine-tip red marker.
Non-toxic glue.

Step one: Take the fortune cookie out of its wrapper.
Step two: Take tweezers and remove the fortune.
Step three: Cut a fortune-sized piece of paper.
Step four: Take your fine-tip marker and write:
You will go steady with Jonny. And you will love him.
Step five: Put the paper in the fortune cookie.
Step six: Put the fortune cookie in the wrapper.
Step seven: Glue the wrapper shut.
Step eight: Give to fortune cookie to Dora.
Step nine: Run like hell.

Context: Montreal

You move to Montreal because you have to. You need the bars to stay open later. You need to experiment. You need purpose, but it must be somewhat attractive. You need cocaine and whisky.

You need a teaching gig. You need to write another book. You need attention. You need last call. You need menthol cigarettes.

You need something to help you fall asleep. You need full sentences, narratives, failure, and full stops.

Jonny's Mid-life Crisis Report: Entry #1

Please help the cause against loneliness,
   Would you like to note my home address?

4310 St. Urbain Street. Basement Bachelor Suite (#1B). Montreal, QC.

My mid-life crisis happens. I leave Dora, my wife of ten years. I move a few blocks away so that I can still be part of my son's life. I move to a basement bachelor apartment on St. Urbain where I will continue to write my little humour pieces. I will convince myself after a few days that I am doing this all for my art. But now, in a peculiar moment of lucidity, I realize the truth is even more selfish than that. It's hard to think about, harder to write about, but I think I want to regress. I think I need to.

The project I am trying to write is called *Stripmalling* — a humorous novel about the life of my anti-hero Jonny, who lives in his Chevette, in the Regent Park strip mall parking lot. The problem with fiction is that the truth is revealed so slowly. Perhaps that's why it's good therapy. But the problem with me is that I spill. Perhaps that's why I'm not a good writer. But how can one develop patience, discipline, and restraint without becoming conservative? I leave home because I fear growing old. I want to write myself younger, with less at stake and less broken.

Luna comes round and I give her a set of keys. She is too beautiful for me. I know this. And she will figure this out soon. She is a singer in a local band called Pleather, and she works at a nightclub and is the object of endless male attention. She will leave me, or I will leave her, and then I will change my locks. Because beautiful people are psychos. But the thing is that fate has been conspiring to bond us. Every time we met in the spring, it would start raining gently, and I would grab her and kiss her under low-hanging trees and in storefront doorways. It was very romantic, and perfect, and lovely. She tells me that she doesn't love me, and I half believe her, and I am half sober.

Luna and I break up after a couple of months. She accidentally had sex with a roadie. Not just any roadie either, a roadie who writes poetry about being a roadie. Last year, he apparently self-published a chapbook of verse called *The Gentle Roadie*. She needed to feel free. She needed to rid herself of the constrictions of a relationship with all of its power dynamics and "rules." I am actually almost crying which is a triumph of sorts, considering the antidepressants I'm on practically have a "No more tears!" guarantee.

"Do you understand how upset this makes me?" I ask, as I fashion a tiny noose out of the phone cord. "I mean, a ROADIE? How did you score that one, Luna? That's an exclusive club you've joined. Seriously. Did you read a book on power seduction? I mean, Jesus Christ!"

"It was actually pretty easy. But Spike is a really tender, loving, and smart person. He's a writer, Jonny. Just like you! But listen, I'm upset too," she says, backstage from her gig in Moose Jaw. "I totally didn't mean it."

"You didn't mean to have sex with your roadie?"

"No. I meant that part. But I didn't mean the feelings part."

"What?? Please, Luna. Stop being obtuse."

"What does obtuse mean?"

Jonny's Mid-life Crisis Report: Entry #2

Dora calls less and less. I think she is feeling less and less hurt. For some reason, I am offended. I call her at 4 A.M. if someone isn't over, and I know that's wrong because she has to be up with Jackson by 6 or 7 A.M. But she answers. And I tell her I miss her and I miss Jackson. Which is true. But it is still evil for me to say. Especially at 4 A.M.

Stripmalling is even more disastrous than my relationships. I don't like the Jonny character. He is weak and not very clever. The Dora character makes a mockery of liberated people who probably deserve better. And Jonny makes fun of the disabled and the well-adjusted. He is the opposite of sympathetic. I will press on though. It's best not to be fond of your characters anyways, because then you let them off the hook.

I think I am a writer now because I wrote one book that some people enjoyed. It's called *Asthmatronics*, and it's a book of lame comedy bits about a fictional version of myself. Jonny. The geeky, asthmatic anti-hero. I know the mild success of the book has gone to my head. I know that people who didn't have the time of day for me before are all of a sudden very friendly. I know that I know better. But still I act like I'm the one kid on the block who has a swimming pool. And I take advantage of all this new attention. And now I want to please people even more with some sort of ambitious, fresh novel. I can tell it's a kind of sickness.

The Dora Report: Entry #1

He's been speaking for me in print since he started to scrawl. Jonny is a foolish man. I do love him. But I can't stand him. I really can't. I don't know how much you will be able to take his revisionist personal mythologies. But here's the truth: he never really lived in his Chevette for more than two days. He tells people it was months, or years, or whatever. The thing about people like Jonny is that they always lose track of their lies. They aren't clever enough to be sociopaths. Of course I took him in. He was so pathetic, so lost. And I'm a huge sucker for a project.

And here's some more truth: Jonny is a part-time instructor at a mildly respectable university, plus he freelances, and drinks his life away. I am a full-time professor at a much better university, a research scientist, and a full-time mother. Jonny isn't a deadbeat dad, but he walks a fine line. He is self obsessed and self-injurious. God help him.

And I don't have a lazy eye. What an asshole.

Hotboxing the Station

Sandy Sev knocked on the glass. I signalled that I would be a minute. It was my first night working alone at the gas station. I had skimmed a good thirty dollars off customers who needed their propane tanks filled. It was a simple scam — I would just lean on the scale a little and the tank would appear completely full to the customer. It was a dirty trick and whenever I looked at my propane license I got a little sad, and then a little hungry, and then a little aroused. The propane license represented the first test I had passed since I cheated my way through Grade 12 Remedial Math.

Anyways, I had my thirty bucks, and I had just finished counting the cigarettes and motor oil. I balanced my shift within two dollars and I was ready to hot box the mother-fucking station. I let Sandy Sev in and she placed three fat joints on the counter. She explained the variety of pot strains, "This one is BC Chronic; this one is Indo-Moroccan Sub-Rainbow Crush, and this, this one is simply called X Factor."

"Nice!" I said. I slipped Sandy fifteen dollars and I took a good long look at her. She was in her late thirties, quite short and plump, and married with three children. She had a quiet confidence that seemed to say: "Hey, just because I'm Ukrainian, doesn't mean I'm going to wax." No one around the strip mall could pronounce her last name. It was a ghastly mix of consonants and when she pronounced it, it sounded like a Klingon curse. We all called her Sandy Sev because she worked at the Sev and we were all very clever with monikers. (They called me Jonny Gaspumper.)

We smoked the BC Chronic first. The mini booth that was the Shill gas station fogged up with sweet leafy goodness. Sandy was perky and charming as we talked about the finer points of retail life. Wasn't it so annoying when customers fiddled around looking for exact change? Wouldn't it be great to win on a scratch ticket and just tell our store managers to fuck off and go to Grand Beach for the summer with a big bag of weed? Next we inhaled the Indo-Moroccan Sub-Rainbow Crush. I fumbled for my inhaler and took five shots of Ventolin. Sandy was beginning to look less repellant. Her light brown upper lip hair matched the wavy hair on her head that had been teased up at the front like that fat lead singer from Heart. Sandy wore her 200 pounds as well as any five-foot-two woman possibly could. And her acid wash jeans and jean jacket were out of style, to be sure, but harkened back to a simpler time when Judas Priest resided in every tape deck and angel dust was plentiful throughout Winnipeg. It was getting harder to breathe in my little booth, but this was a celebration. Sandy Sev lit up the X Factor as soon as the Indo-Moroccan Sub-Rainbow Crush was cashed.

I am a firm believer that drugs are never an excuse for bad behaviour. But I am also a firm believer that the X

Factor joint was laced with some amour-inducing agent, like ecstasy, cocaine, or Ajax. Before I knew it, my lips were locked with Sandy Sev's. "What about your girlfriend?" she squealed urgently.

"Dora? She doesn't have much luck with threesomes. I'll call her later," I said, as I shoved my tongue down Sandy's throat.

She tasted of cabbage rolls and Craven Menthol cigarettes. Sweet Sandy Sev. I tried to take her in my arms, but I pulled a muscle in my forearm and almost collapsed. She took charge, shoved me against the window and we slid down to the floor together in a heap of sweaty passion. As we rolled around the recently mopped floor I had a pang of lucidity: the cloud of smoke was at best a temporary curtain. We should have bailed from the station, and gone somewhere more private, like a Motel 6, a youth hostel, or a back alley.

I regained my composure and willed my erection away as I stumbled behind the counter. "Okay, Sandy. I'm gonna set the alarm, so go wait in your van and I will be right with you."

"You got it, pumper," she said.

As she opened the door the smoke cleared out and my head cleared a little as well. Not completely though, I looked at Sandy as she sashayed out. I was still gonna tap that. I double-checked the vault, the till, and the cigarettes. All good. I made sure the propane was shut off. Yep. I was ready to rock, and rock Sandy Sev's world. I looked up and saw that Sandy had unbuttoned her Sev shirt and was flashing me from the door. I gave her a little wink and motioned for her to stand clear. It was time to set the alarm. I pressed the "Alarm Set" button and activated the code. I had twenty seconds to leave the station and lock up. BEEP BEEP BEEP . . . I hurried my way to the door, and slipped on Sandy Sev's DD bra. My head collided with the metal handle of the door and I lay in a crumpled heap. BEEP BEEP BEEP . . . I could hear Sandy screaming and banging on the door. BANG BANG BANG . . . BEEP BEEP BEEP. And as I stumbled to my feet, the alarm went off. I lunged toward the alarm console to deactivate the alarm, but I couldn't recall the code. 5194? 5149? 9154? Stupid three varieties of pot! My lust for life was ruining my professional life!

Sandy and I locked eyes and then she bailed. I was abandoned and the cops were surely on their way. I did the only thing I could. I made a handsome decorative wreath out of Sandy Sev's DD bra and stumbled out into the cold Winnipeg night, to my Chevette and its comforting block heater. And for one night, I would find another strip mall parking lot to sleep in.

Jonny's Mid-life Crisis Report: Entry #3

Jackson grows up, and I watch from a safe distance because I feel contagious in the worst sense of the word. I don't want my son to catch my self-abuse, my self-doubt, and my self-loathing. He is curious and kind-hearted. Not shy at all. I don't want him to be an artist. A research scientist would be perfect. Like his mother. I don't mean to suggest that artists are tortured souls, or that it's a tough life and we are so hard done by, or anything like that; it's just that we are not very good people.

It's almost not fair to call this a mid-life crisis; it's a preemptive mid-life crisis. I am only thirty-one. But, on the other hand, it could be considered a three-quarter-life crisis because I am drinking my way to a very early grave. I will be dead by forty unless I convert to some weird-ass, obscure religion like Christianity and start treating my body like a temple. Right now I treat my body like a youth hostel with a well-deserved bad reputation.

I think *Stripmalling* will follow a dialogic structure where my stories will be interspersed with journal entries documenting my mid-life crisis. Maybe that's my way out. I'm not very fond of things happening in stories. Mine is a static literature. I have realized that I can't write myself younger; I just wonder if I can write myself back home. Home is where the strip mall is.

The Dora Report: Entry #2

Jonny always got what he wanted. I don't know if there's a word for someone like that — you know, someone who is capable of anything, but thinks he is incapable of everything. I think the closest clinical term would be "idiot."

But the truth is, from the first time I saw that guy in his ratty Ramones T-shirt, selling hash from his hatchback to thirteen-year-old skater kids, I had a special feeling. He was too shy to talk to me, but he wouldn't stop staring. So I initiated a pattern that would continue to this day. I took pity on him and helped him feel better about himself, helped him get the job at the Shill station, gave him a place to shower and shave.

He was so fearful. Why would he put himself in such a situation? I bet he won't even tell the important shit about the strip mall. I hope he does, and I hope he doesn't. He breaks my heart. Jonny was a dealer for Sandy Sev. Sandy supplied the weed, hash, and coke in the strip mall, and on the weekends, she would volunteer at the drop-in centre. Fucking hypocrite. Anyways, if Jonny doesn't tell you what happened to our strip mall then I will. Deal?

It's Hard to Get Fired from a Gas Station, but I'm Special

"Tuck in that shirt," Mr. Stubler would say.

"No," I would say.

That's the kind of relationship we had. Mr. Stubler was an ex-minor pro hockey player with a Napoleon complex. He always talked about how he would have made more money and would have broken into the NHL if it weren't for the widely held bias against players under five foot seven.

"I had mad skills!" Mr. Stubler would suddenly shout out. "I had hands. Oh boy, did I have good hands! I could dangle. I mean really dangle, boy."

It was always a good policy to ignore Mr. Stubler's Tourettic bursts of bitter nostalgia. But sometimes I could not hold back. I was in a particularly good mood when I blew up at Mr. Stubler. I had spent the whole morning stealing money from propane customers, and between customers, I wrote what I considered to be a very successful comedy bit called "Voice Mails to Helen Keller."

It practically wrote itself: "Hello? Helen? Why won't you answer? WAKE THE FUCK UP! I'm trying to COM-MUNICATE with you!" I was still developing my voice, but this was a huge step forward. Pure gold.

"Jonny, what did I tell you about tucking in your shirt?" Stubler asked.

"Sorry Mr. Stubler. I forget. Remind me again. Are you pro- or anti-tuck?"

"Don't push it, Jonny Gaspumper. I'm in no mood."

"Sigh." I tucked in my shirt, and, as soon as he turned his back, I untucked it again.

I always had trouble with jocks and ex-jocks like Stubler. They treated everyone the way their coaches treated them. It was a kind of "eyes on the prize" / "in it to win it" mentality. And since there was no prize in the life of a gas jockey, it was very hard to buy in.

When I was around ten or so, I was a second line left-winger for the Oxford Heights Community Club Blues. I was having a decent season: a few goals and assists, and was fairly well-regarded among my teammates despite my early penchant for breaking out into show tunes in the dressing room. I quickly learned to curb that behaviour. Most ten-year-old boys from Transcona were not as interested in the work of Andrew Lloyd Webber as I was. Oh sure, there was a significant number of older gentleman who were Andrew Lloyd Webber fans and interested in ten-year-old boys, but that's a different story. I did my best to conceal my more feminine interests from the other children. I loved Strawberry Shortcake, My Little Pony, and Care Bears, but that was to remain a secret from my sporting comrades.

My father was surprisingly eager to facilitate my love for the gentler toys of '80s kid culture. So long as I promised to remain enrolled in baseball, football, and hockey, Dad would purchase the most wonderful dollhouses and cuddly pink things for me. He told me I had to keep it on the "down-low." He told me that as I grew up to be a man, I would learn the profound importance of keeping certain special things on the "down-low." I wasn't entirely sure what he was getting at, but I appreciated the toys.

One mid-December evening, Dad took me to Consumers Distributing to pick up my most coveted product: Cheer Bear. The pink Care Bear with the adorable rainbow across his stomach. Cheer Bear was my absolute favourite. As we approached the counter, Dad whispered to me, "Don't make a scene, Jonny. Remember the down-low."

But as the cashier handed over the Cheer Bear, my enthusiasm took over. "I love you, Cheer Bear! You're super awesome!" I said, as I clutched the pink thing close to my heart. My dad nudged me toward the door, and I found myself face to face with eleven-year-old Bryan Finnegan, centre of the second line for the Oxford Heights Community Club Blues, almost five feet and a very good puck handler, and quite unsympathetic when it came to cultural choices that challenged conventional gender roles.

"Oh . . . my . . . fucking . . . God!" said Bryan, sounding like a prepubescent Charlton Heston. "Jonny, is that your little pink teddy bear?"

His mom gave him a gentle slap. "Leave the sissy boy alone, Bry," she said.

"Yeah. Don't fuck with Cheer Bear, Bryan. If you know what's good for you," I said. Dad had already bailed on me and I could see him running toward the car like he had just been busted for shoplifting. I guess the jig was up.

"Oh, I won't fuck with your teddy bear, Jonny. Don't worry," Bryan said as his mom dragged him off to the Sporting Goods department. I will always remember his face as I slowly backed out of the doorway. His freckles were lost in the pink glow of his blushing pudgy face. He was equally embarrassed for me, and delighted for himself. "Jonny has a teddy bear!" he taunted as he disappeared.

My production as a left-winger for the Oxford Heights Community Club Blues dwindled from that point. I was dropped from the second line to the fourth and even there I found it difficult to get anyone to pass to me, even if I was wide open, cherry-picking at centre ice. The nickname "Queer Bear" stuck for years, and I slowly withdrew from all organized sports. The retreat from the community club to the bedroom was a painful one and I will never forgive Bryan Finnegan for "othering" me. I was only trying to "trouble" conventional expectations of gender, or something like that.

And I guess that was the thing about Mr. Stubler. A slightly taller, slightly less mature version of Bryan Finnegan — that's all he was. Sandy Sev came into the station to buy some menthol cigarettes, and I flirted with her for a little bit. Stubler was watching me from the office — watching to see if I would attend to the Dodge Caravan that had pulled up for gas, or whether I would continue to entertain Sandy with my spot-on Stubler impression.

"Jonny, get pumping that van!" Stubler screamed. So I slipped Sandy a free pack of smokes, winked, and jumped to the pump. Unfortunately on my way out, my shirt got caught in the door. As I struggled to free myself, Stubler strode up to me with an evil look on his garden gnome face. There we stood, man-to-hobbit, and then he let me have it. "Jonny, you are a useless hump. You know that?"

"Hump, sir?"

"Listen, you are a HUMP. A fucktarded little fuckface hump."

"Fucktarded, sir?"

"Just forget it. Turn in your name tag. Your ass is fired, motherfucker."

I was devastated. Sweat started pouring down my face, and tears slowly formed in my ducts. The strip mall was my home. And I needed the job to pay for my extravagant lifestyle! And Dora? She would never date a jobless wonder. She had standards! "Oh yeah, Stubler? Well you are a shitty-ass boss, and you were a shitty-ass hockey player. You couldn't even stay in the minors, you . . . you . . . HUMP!"

I regretted that outburst as soon as I said it. For as good as it felt to let Stubler have it with my superior linguistic abilities, it really fucking hurt when he let loose a flying Gordie Howe–style elbow to my head, freeing me from the door and landing me on the sidewalk outside. Sandy Sev stepped over my twitching body on her way out. "Oh, Jonny," she said, "you are one special little shit."

Jonny's Mid-life Crisis Report: Entry #4

"I'm gonna be a pornographer. I'm gonna make pornography!" my brother, Jamie, declares. "Do I need to spell it out for you? P-O-R-N . . . et cetera."

"Jesus, Jamie!" I say.

"Watch your mouth, Jonny," my father said.

My mom, dad, Jamie, and I are all in a rental car, heading to Brooklyn. I'm in New York to launch *Asthmatronics*. My brother has lived in the Bronx for the last seven years, after leaving Winnipeg, and his garage band life, behind him. He had been trying to "make it" as a Satan-worshipping, Latino rap artist. He rapped under the name "Rubio." He still holds a weekend job, directing a choir at a Catholic church. My parents are in New York to intermediate between Jamie and his soon-to-be ex-wife, Gigi. You see, as Jamie's career in Satanic/Hispanic hip hop fizzled, his first love, internet pornography, has re-emerged, and it is now sapping him of all of his artistic energy.

Anyway, since we are all in New York for good reasons, we decided to make my Brooklyn book launch a family outing. I suppose I'm being selfish, but I think it's unfair of Jamie to pick this time, en route to my first professional New York City appearance as an author, to announce his career shift. Dad is praying and driving at the same time. He's never been that great of a multi-tasker, and he misses the Williamsburg Bridge. My eyes are locked on the clock on the radio. We have an hour to spare. And I had been hoping to get to the cabaret early enough to rehearse my hilarious bits and have at least ten shots of Jägermeister to calm the old nerves.

"Porn is the new art!" Jamie says. "Anyways, I'm trading in professional Satan worship for porn. As far as you're concerned, it's a step in the right direction."

I close my eyes and bite my tongue. "Turn left here, Dad. You can double back to the bridge."

Then Mom chirps in: "Have you asked yourself WWJD, Jamie?"

"He'd probably try to find hot chicks to film, especially if his wife was leaving him," Jamie responds.

I'm pretty sure that Jamie assumes that WWJD does not stand for "What would Jesus do?" but for "What would Jamie do?" or "What would John Stamos do?"

I'm almost thirty, I think to myself. And here I am being driven to my own book launch as if it were fucking soccer practice! What the hell was I thinking? I could have taken the L train like all the other writers! When we get to the venue, an ultra-hip bar in the ultra-hip area of Williamsburg, I go straight for the merch table. As I set up my books, the lead singer of the 8 P.M.-scheduled band, Soul Cracker, takes his CDs away. He looks like a balder, more intellectually challenged version of Dave Matthews. Needless to say, he isn't swamped with hangers-on. So I ask how his gig went.

"Harsh, man. New York is a tough nut to crack." He has obviously been on tour for ten years, ever since that period in the mid-'90s where his plaid pajama pants represented the height of fashion. I trade him a book for a CD, knowing full well that the CD will go unheard, the book unskimmed.

A few hipsters trickle in to the club. As I try to schmooze, I hear my mom bellow, "Jonny, dear, introduce us to your new friends!"

"Shut up, Mom. Jonny's trying to act cool," Jamie says.

I shudder, bite my lip, and press on. I had a hilarious set to prepare.

Most of the hipsters who have shown up turn out to be fellow performers in the cabaret-style show that has been planned. I'm to follow the Brazilian folk dance duo, who have basically just taken off their clothes and convulsed onstage for ten minutes. How can I follow that? As they get offstage I glimpse Jamie giving them his business card. At least one transaction will be made this night.

I mount the stage and quickly launch into my comedy bit, a touching story about a young asthmatic boy making love to a vacuum cleaner. My Canadian-specific references are lost on them. They don't know who Anne of Green Gables is, and they aren't interested in how her hypothetical heroin addiction may be quite hilarious, or at least change our collective world view. All of my jokes are bombing, even my off-the-cuff Burt Reynolds impression and my spontaneous spoken-word version of "Ghostbusters." I look out into the audience and I see my family: Mom, Dad, and Jamie; they are the only ones laughing and at all appropriate cues! They are being as supportive as possible. It's like I am Celine Dion, and, collectively, my family is that creepy old René guy. I feel a flood of emotions. Good ones! I have to pay tribute to them. And I do so in the only way I know: I screw them over.

I abandon my book and point out my family to the audience. I tell everyone the story of the ride down. My brother's broken marriage, the imminent pornography ring, my parents' religious zealotry, my own whiny sense of entitlement. I embellish liberally. My dad becomes Donald Rumsfeld, my mom becomes Tammy Faye Bakker, and Jamie becomes a combination of Larry Flynt and Gene Simmons. Now everyone in the bar is laughing except my family. Now I'm killing! I end my rant to uproarious applause, and, later that night, I even sell some books! I realize that my family has provided me with a wonderful gift: a deep well of subject matter from an even deeper reservoir of shame. And more specifically, on this particular night, they enable me to reclaim my stage and escape the fate of dying in Brooklyn.

You Can't Put a Price on Poverty

Dora and I moved into an apartment in downtown Winnipeg. It was a '60s-style modern high-rise building shaped like a milk carton with yellow and blue stripes on each side. It looked just like every other building in Winnipeg. We had a one-bedroom and cats named Conan and Andy. We had indoor parking for the Chevette and a wall-unit air conditioner. We were practically yuppies! Except we had no money and we couldn't afford the place. Dora's beloved Libby's Discount Fabrics had been demolished, and the strip mall was going through some severe growing pains. The American super store, Hypermart, had purchased seventy-five percent of the mall. The fabric store, arcade, hockey card shop, Chinese takeout, were all gone. The Shill station remained. Dora made the lateral move from night manager at Libby's to night manager of the Housewares section at Hypermart. Everyday she would drive my Chevette from the anachronistic wasteland of downtown Winnipeg to the really anachronistic wasteland of strip mall world — downtown Transcona.

Dora would ask how my writing was coming along and I would get angry. Jack Nicholson angry. Carol Channing angry. Angry angry. "Listen, Dora. I am not about to unleash this stuff on the world. It would blow people's minds. Workers would quit; democracy would crumble; no one would bother reading again; the laws of physics would be reversed; puppies would unleash themselves on us and form provisional governments! And I'm not willing to serve a puppy-authored agenda. Are you? Because if I show you, you will show others, and that's how minds get blown. That's how *minds get blown,* do you hear me, Dora?"

Of course it was just pure cowardice on my part. My poetic tributes to Imipramine, my contra-puppy pamphlets, my comedy bits about people with disabilities were not quite ready to share with other people. The truth was, I wasn't a very good writer. I didn't know a gerund from a transitive verb. I still don't. But I feel much more comfortable using such terms freely now. I explained to Dora that my writing would require as much free time as possible. So no, I wouldn't be going to Mr. Stubler and begging for my job back. And no, I wouldn't be applying for any jobs or paper routes. And for the last time yes, I *was* too busy to shower and brush my teeth every day. God, women just don't understand the suffering one must endure in the name of art.

I would tease my brain by subjecting it to *Star Trek* novels that continued the five-year mission of Captain Kirk and his gang. I would rent videos of *The Flintstones* for insight into the American family (one of my primary literary interests), and still Dora would question my dedication to writing. It was infuriating. And yes, still, once a week, Dora would ask to see my journals. I resorted to getting a small chest at Value Village and three bicycle locks to secure my new writer's chest.

Some nights I would wait until Dora was sleeping then take the elevator down to the parkade and sleep in the back of the Chevette. I would look over my notes. I would sing myself to sleep by crooning Ramones songs in half whispers. The truth was, I was depressed and afraid of living in the real world.

In the winter, I lost a part of me when I sold the Chevette to make December's rent. I was having trouble getting used to being poor. And like they say, you can't put a price on poverty. I think they say that. I'm pretty sure. Not that I was ever rich growing up, but I was middle-class enough to understand that I wasn't poor. I had all the Care Bears and Strawberry Shortcakes a confused young boy could possibly need. I had posters of Paula Abdul and Pauly Shore. I had everything I desired. Except friends.

Dora and I lived in a world of NSF fees and postdated late rent cheques. Of dollar-store dinners and collection agency phone calls. Dora had shifted her focus from polyamory to vegetarianism. I was right behind her on this one. No more meat. Together we would beat meat. Or something like that.

As the winter passed like a slow-moving ice-type thing, I was having some minor breakthroughs. But these were more like comedy bits. "Dubious Toasts" was a delicious bit of business that consisted of inappropriate things to raise a glass to: "Here's to the human vagina! Of all the vaginas I've tried, this one really gets the job done!" or, "Here's to Charles M. Dentaldam, inventor of the dental dam! You saved us all buddy!" or, "Here's to the invasion of Poland! We'll get 'em next time!"

Or some of my other classic comedy routines like "Babies with Tourette's," which involved a whole lotta babies cussing, and "Freudian Scat," which involved a jazz scat singer accidentally saying horrible things in the middle of a scat. That last one didn't translate too well to the page. But I still think it's gold. I'm not sure why but a lot of my writing involved people saying horrible things. I guess it's because horrible things are funny. Also, I couldn't write a sentence without an exclamation point. I guess exclamation points are funny too.

One day I was people-watching at the arcade, and also playing *Star Wars* pinball. But mostly people-watching. It was research. You know, for the writing. I came home around 11 P.M., a half-hour before Dora's shift at Hypermart ended. But for some reason she was home early. She was dressed in a revealing yet tasteful light blue negligee, and there was a vintage seafoam green typewriter on the coffee table with a big red bow on it.

"Surprise!" she gurgled. "I bought it at Value Village!"

"The negligee?

"No, you fucking moron, the typewriter!"

"It's amazing!" I looked it over. It was from the '70s or

something. Real cool looking and all the keys worked too.

"It's a gesture of my belief in you. I know you're going to make it as a writer. I have no doubt. I don't need to see your work, and I'm sorry I've been pushing so hard. I just want you to know I believe in you."

I was speechless. It was a long moment. A tumbleweed moment. It was more like an hour than a moment. It took a long time. Then I took off my pants. And Dora sighed and put on her pajamas.

The next day I went to the University of Winnipeg, armed with Dora's library card, and I took out two books: Roland Barthes' *The Pleasure of the Text,* and *The Collected Mark Twain.* You see, in the light of day, I realized that Dora's gift was a gesture of faith, but it was equally a challenge: *So you're a writer eh? You're going to sit on the couch all day waiting for the muses to goose you while I earn the money to pay the bills? Fine. So prove it. Prove you can write. And get to fucking work already.*

After reading through Twain and scratching my head through Barthes, I typed out a greatly exaggerated resumé and went down the Hypermart that had colonized the old Regent Park strip mall, where I applied for a job as a cashier. Dora was my only reference. On a grey, frigid morning, Dora and I took the 47 bus to Transcona and my job interview. As we got off the bus and trudged toward the old strip mall, the images rushed back. The petrol-soaked, super-stoned afternoons and evenings at the Shill station. The harmless, victimless petty theft. The beatings.

"So, Jonny, I see that you worked as a research assistant for a pharmaceutical company. Can you tell me a little about that experience?" Mr. Hardman asked.

"Oh sure. Well, I mostly just did drugs, you know. It was mostly on a volunteer basis, but my colleague, Sandy, would supply the pharmaceuticals and conduct very rigorous experiments on things like motor skills and sex drive."

"I see. Well, your resumé is a little incomplete. What was the name of the company?"

"Uhh. Spliff Technologies."

"Right. So you did a lot of drugs with Sandy, then?"

"You know Sandy Sev?"

"Where do you think I get my Sub-Moroccan Rainbow Crush?" He smiled.

I was hired.

Jonny's Mid-life Crisis Report: Entry #5

The moderate success of *Asthmatronics* has taken me to some amazing places. I am now writing *Stripmalling* from Russia. I am here in St. Petersburg, lecturing on contemporary literary humour. I have been thinking about having an affair with a Russian woman, but I think I am too shy, or afraid, or something. Plus there is a strange cultural divide that prevents Russian women from finding me attractive. They all scowl at me. It makes me pine for home where the women just roll their eyes, or, on a good night, humour me. Russia is like this weird planet that they might visit on an episode of *Star Trek* where all of the aliens only speak Russian.

If I were to have a Russian affair, I would like to have one with a clever, manipulative arts administrator called Annika. And if I were to have such an affair, Annika would take me to hip St. Petersburg clubs where boys and girls in fauxhawks and mullets would dance to American surf guitar until seven in the morning, drinking Baltika 7 beer and vodka, and snorting coke in dirty unisex washrooms.

Annika would be hyper-assured of her future in New York as a curator and she would outwit me with her rudimentary English and I would cheat and tell her that she was using the wrong idioms, and she would apologize, and I would feel slightly less stupid. Annika would ask me to promise not to write her into my novel, and I would say, "I promise."

We would hold hands and stroll down Nevsky Prospect — Nevsky Prospect is a peculiar street with amazing, classic European architecture. Monuments to Peter the Great, Pushkin, Nabokov, Anna Akhmatova abound. Stone buildings of remarkable beauty now house franchises like KFC, Subway, McDonald's, The Gap, Pizza Hut. The stripmalling of Russia. Take that, Dostoevsky.

Jonny's Mid-life Crisis Guide to St. Petersburg

People ask me all the time: "Jonny, what will you write when *Stripmalling* is done?" And I always give the same answer: travel writing. Travel writing is how we get to intimately know other cultures and judge them. Travel writing is what separates us from lesser creatures like apes and the Flemish. And, inevitably, travel writing will ensure the security of our nation (Canada) and its people. There is a global war on terror and it's time we woke up, put on our pants, had a little nosh, and got familiar with a big old bastard known as the Red Menace. So with all this in mind, I am proud to present my first ever stab at travel writing, *Jonny's Mid-life Crisis Guide to St. Petersburg*. It's possibly the most essential text you will ever read, so you might want to sit down, take a deep breath, and apply a liberal amount of ointment to wherever there is irritation.

The City

St. Petersburg was founded in 1941 by an ex-merchant Marine named Peter Parker. He was such an awesome guy, and really cool to drink with and so all the local people called him "Peter the Awesome." He had a short temper, however, and he forcibly shaved off the beards of every Russian woman who lived in the city. He killed Finnish people for sport and was an excellent bowler. The city was originally named St. Petersbourg, but the *O* was soon dropped when Peter the Awesome deemed it too sexually suggestive. When the Germans attacked in 1988 the city was renamed Hasselhoffgrad. It was renamed recently when a drunk David Hasselhoff appeared in an embarrassing video on the internet. To this day, the people of St. Petersburg are excellent bowlers and not particularly good at making love.

The Neva River

When Peter the Awesome founded St. Petersburg, he decided to build an entire river, complete with many canals and tourist trap river boats with video lottery terminals on board. Peter wanted to distinguish the Neva from all those other boring rivers he had swam in as a child. So he ordered that, instead of water, the Neva be filled with Fresca, a refreshing, carbonated soda beverage. When it was discovered that Fresca could not stay carbonated in the open air, Peter became enraged and shot many Finns. The Neva, of course, was named after American actress Neve Campbell.

The Hermitage

The Hermitage is the world's largest old folks' home. There's some art on the walls. It is a favourite of tourists from far and wide even though there are a lot of old people in it. It features the world's longest game of shuffleboard and smells very, very bad.

The Rick Astley Monument

Like so many aliens on *Star Trek*, Rick Astley is a being of pure energy and is capable of instant matter regeneration. He has always been, and always will be. He was so many great men in our history: Plato, Churchill, JFK, Lincoln, and of course, Rick Astley. When the people of St. Petersburg first heard "Never Gonna Give You Up," they knew instantly that Astley was the real fucking deal. The Astley Monument is located on Nevsky Prospekt and features a gigantic statue of a pleated-jeans-and-cardigan-sweater-wearing Astley drinking a bottle of Diet Pepsi. Looking good, Rick Astley, looking real good.

The Church of the Spilled Blood

Once, while summering with John Travolta, Jesus went to this now famous church to pray to himself. Travolta got tired of waiting in the beer garden for Jesus, marched into the church, and said, "Hey, Jesus, like c'mon! We gotta split!"

Jesus got super pissed off and drop kicked Travolta in the face.

Travolta's cleft chin burst open and he said, "Aww geez!" Travolta stumbled out onto the steps of the church and he collapsed there, bleeding and crying and in great pain. For Jesus was very powerful and had taken kung-fu lessons.

Jonny's Mid-life Crisis Report: Entry #6

Back now in Montreal. Wondering how to write my way back into *Stripmalling*. Instead I spend time in old haunts on St. Laurent Boulevard. St. Laurent has been written about too much, in small press and large — its status as the Main Street of English Montreal is safe without my contribution to its mythology. Nevertheless, the bars I frequent are all on this strip. Everyone is a writer, or was a writer.

If you want to develop a cocaine habit, or if you want to develop bedsores, Montreal is the place for you. I am attempting to develop a theory about literary writers. It goes something like this: we are all glorified diarists. And although writing itself can be cathartic, or even healthy, the publication of any literary text is unacceptable. It is indicative of some kind of intense pathology. I am currently blaming writing for the breakup of my marriage; it's an easy target — so narcissistic, so deconstructive by nature.

I meet Evan at the worst coke bar in Montreal. It's so transparent, so enmeshed in the drug culture and mythology of Montreal, it's actually called "Le Coke Bar." I watch the local poets and novelists make frequent trips to the stalls to blow away their grey matter. I watch the regulars clutch their Jamesons and 50s and Budweisers, and I clutch my Bud too. Evan jokes about the most inappropriate things, in a gay George Carlin style. He looks like a young, male Isabella Rossellini. A classic beauty with the mouth of a sailor. I am taken and taken home.

When we get to Evan's Parc Avenue apartment, I am stunned by the stacks of comic books and paraphernalia. The walls are covered with Norman Rockwell prints and *X-Men* posters. There are coloured pencils and sketch pads everywhere, superhero figurines serve as paperweights and bookends.

We make out and listen to old records: the Stones, the Stone Roses, Sly and the Family Stone (we were stoned). I decide he will enter me and my novel. His art will carry strategic portions of my narrative. We are looking at each other, somewhat lovingly, in his bed at 5 A.M. I have been telling him about *Stripmalling*. I tell him about how, in my world, everyone is loitering. As the sun rises, we are still tweaked and still talking. He laughs at my comedy bits. The ones long-abandoned, my juvenilia. He promises to illustrate them.

"Jonny?" he says.

"Yes, Evan?"

"I'm pulling for your narrative."

Really Bad Comics

BY JONNY AND EVAN

Dictators and Their Favourite Toys

SADDAM HUSSEIN
CHEER BEAR

KIM JONG IL
STRAWBERRY SHORTCAKE

MUAMMAR AL-GADDAFI
MY LITTLE PONY

RUHOLLAH KHOMEINI
POUND PUPPY

Freudian Scat

Helen Keller's Voice Mail

Dubious Toasts

Babies with Tourette's

Jonny's Mid-life Crisis Report: Entry #7

Jackson is flourishing. It's not entirely surprising. Dora is an exceptionally clever woman and he is very much Dora's son. He has a scientist's curiosity and attention to detail. When I take him to the grocery store, he faces me and tugs at my coat from his safely tethered position in the front of the cart. It's winter and I'm sweating. I haven't had a drink or a smoke today because I am trying to keep that shit out of Jack's sight from now on. I haven't shopped for groceries since last week. Jackson is sleeping over tonight and he needs something to eat.

Jack is two and a half. His eyes dart from one thing to the next. "Whassat?" he says, pointing to various objects of interest.

"Whassat, Daddy?"

"Christmas lights."

"Whassat?"

"All-purpose cleaner."

"Whassat?"

"Uh, condoms, Jackson."

"What's condoms?"

"They are for big people only, Jack."

"'Kay, Daddy."

We wheel past the cooler. The stacks of beer beckon but I push the cart past. Jack is pointing at the twelve-packs and he says, "Look! It's Daddy's medicine!" People stare and I quickly maneuver the cart safely to the cereal aisle. I remember around a year ago, holding a beer in my hand, over Jack's bed. I was trying to give him a dose of Children's Tylenol. And in order to get him to open up I had to illustrate to him that I had to take "Daddy's medicine." It occurs to me now that naming things has consequences.

Jackson is fast asleep on his air mattress. I am in my bedroom and I cannot sleep. I am shaking a little. Withdrawing a little. I stare at the ceiling until it's cartoon time at 6:30 A.M. I only have to go once or twice a week without vice. It's really not that bad.

The Strip Mall Is Dead

Even though he is two years older than me, my brother, Jamie, still lived with my parents. Even as I graduated from Chevette to apartment, and hack writer to published writer, Jamie had his own dreams. He was a drummer in a heavy metal outfit called Satanicus. He would come in Hypermart every once in a while and buy groceries: Doritos, Pepsi, instant noodles, et cetera.

I spent most of my shifts feverishly writing: scrawling poems and jokes on receipt paper. But perhaps the most interesting thing I wrote while on the clock was a list. It was a fairly simple one:

Then

Dora -> Libby's.

Libby -> Libby's.

Henry -> Henry's.

Darren -> Sudsy's.

Jimmy -> Blip's.

Benny Lyons -> A Taste of China.

Robbie Lyons -> A Taste of China.

Sandy Sev -> The Sev.

Me -> Shill.

Now

Dora -> Hypermart Housewares.

Libby -> Hypermart Housewares.

Henry -> Hypermart Hardware.

Darren -> Hypermart Automotive.

Jimmy -> Hypermart Video Centre.

Benny Lyons -> Hypermart Stockroom.

Sandy Sev -> Hypermart Cashier.

Me -> Hypermart Cashier.

Robbie Lyons -> Nowhere.

We wore bright blue smocks and recited a pledge to our company at the beginning of our shift. We were told to smile. We were told to address people as "sir" or "ma'am." We were told that we were a family.

My brother lurked in the personal health aisle by the Hypermart Pharmacy. He was doing lethargic laps around the douches, sponges, anti-fungal agents, and condoms. His long, scraggly hair hid his eyes. I was on my way to the employee lounge for my break. When I saw him, I crouched down at the end of the aisle and watched Jamie closely. I saw him slide two packs of extra large condoms into his trench-coat pocket. This was disturbing for so very many reasons. Just when he thought he was in the clear, I popped out from my hiding spot.

"Can I help you with anything, sir?" I asked.

"Hey, bro. Just um . . . checkin' stuff out, you know?"

"Oh for sure Jamie. I know. Hey listen, here's a hot tip: our topical creams are going to be fifteen percent off next weekend! You might just want to let it itch for a while and save some money, you know?"

"Fuck off, Jonny."

"I saw you take the condoms, Jamie."

Jamie got sweaty and his face turned red. But as he brushed his hair out of his face, I could see that his eyes were defiant. "So, what are you gonna to do about it?" Jamie said.

"What do you think I'm gonna do about it?"

Jamie leaned in and whispered. "Don't be a fucking rat, Jonny. Don't be a fucking rat."

I smiled and put my arm on his shoulder. "Jamie, you may be a total douche, but you are my brother. I wouldn't dream of busting you."

Jamie's mood quickly shifted from anxious to cocky. "I know you won't. Besides what could you possibly do to me? I would kick your ass, you little shit."

"Whatever, Jamie."

Jamie slid by and I quickly made my way to the intercom. My voice bellowed through Hypermart. "Security to the front of the store please."

Restraining my brother was a fantastic feeling. I remembered countless scenes of Jamie pinning me down, giving it to me with spit torture, titty twisters, noogies, and other things that are too embarrassing even for fiction. Benny from the stockroom was kicking Jamie in the gut as I pinned his arms down with my knees. Now I was on top, and Jamie tasted my wrath and my spit. It was one of the best moments of my life. When Jamie started to cry, I felt a wave of empathy envelop me. This was, after all, my brother. I told Benny to run and get the manager. And when Benny was out of sight, I looked into Jamie's eyes. "I'm gonna let you go now, Jamie. But remember, you owe me one, okay?"

"I'm gonna fucking kill you!"

"Well, if you're gonna be unreasonable about it, then I can just hold you down until Mr. Hardman comes." I was stronger than Jamie now. That's the trick time plays on older brothers. They can bully all they want, but at some point, the younger brother grows into an adult body and it's payback time.

"Fine! I owe you one."

As I watched Jamie limp off into the evening with his wounded pride and his extra large condoms, I felt that I had done the right thing. Family first.

The Dora Report: Entry #3

That obviously never happened. And it's not even a good story. But it is true, however, that Jamie needs extra large condoms.

Something strange is going on with Jonny. I mean, not stranger than the pre-emptive mid-life crisis and leaving his wife and son, but more unlike him. He keeps telling me there is more to his story. And he is keeping it from me. He hasn't done that since we were young. He lets me read everything. He insists upon it. But now, apparently, he is working on a "special part of the book" that he won't let me in on. I don't know if I believe him. But I guess he is more and more prone to keeping me out.

Jonny's Mid-life Crisis Report: Entry #8

Something strange is going on with me. Suki Schroeder is the girl who has effectively ended my mid-life crisis, or at least my desire to continue my mid-life crisis. She's a unique blend of German and Japanese, and she has an intellectual curiosity that seems to know no bounds. She drills me on theories of comedic expression in literary contexts. She wants to fuck all the time, which is at once refreshing and draining.

She slides into my apartment after drinking with her fellow graduate students, and she forces her opinions on me and she forces herself on me. And I am pleased for a while. Fucking Suki Schroeder is like nothing I've ever experienced. She is fluent in English, Japanese, and German, and she will shift between all three during sex. One minute it's all: *"Shiko shiko suru! Kuso! Omae o korosu! Mikosurihan! Yowaily!"* The next minute it's all: *"Ich will dich ficken! Fick Dich! Frühspritzer!"* And by the third minute, I'm usually asleep, and she's smoking a cigarette. Being with Suki Schroeder is like some sort of weird psychosexual Second World War nightmare. But for some reason, you don't really want to wake up. You want to see how it ends.

Lately, I have been having trouble coming. I don't have a problem getting it up, it's just I can't seem to finish. It's

3 A.M. Suki knocks on the window of my basement apartment and I wearily make my way to the front entrance to let her in. She wants to fuck. She's coked up, and more than a little drunk. Her hair smells like a mix of apple shampoo and herbal cigarettes. Her tongue tastes of Jameson and Mentos. She paws at me. "C'mon, Jonny. Let's fuck."

I try to deflect. "Why won't you tell your classmates that we are a couple?"

"We've been over this a billion fucking times, Jonny. You are a pedagogue. You teach at the university. I am a student. You are in a position of power, an evaluative position. You put me at an immediate disadvantage. And I will not be thrust into a position of potential scorn or micropolitical peril."

"I don't teach you. I only teach undergrads. And we're the same age for Chrissakes! There's no imbalance. There's no political fallout."

"Jonny, listen to me. You hoard my desire. You are in complete control. This whole situation is way too Lacanian already."

"What does that even mean? I think you are ashamed of me."

"Shame is certainly a key component in this problematic."

"Is problematic actually a noun as well?"

"Yes."

"Are you sure?"

"Yeah. I just wikipedia-ed it the other day."

"You know that's not a valid source."

"Trust me."

Suki bites my neck. Hard. And then all discussion ends, and she takes over. To me, it's clear she's in charge. After twenty minutes or so of awkward fucking, Suki climbs on top of me and uses the second shelf of my IKEA bookcase for leverage. In her drunken exuberance, she shakes the bookshelf too hard and the top row of *Asthmatronics* comes tumbling down on both of us. We are covered in multiple copies of my moderately successful comedy book. Suki bursts into laughter and I take the opportunity to switch positions. I move behind her. As I fuck her from behind, I look at the books strewn on the futon. I start reading the blurbs on the back. They say I am "An exciting young writer," "A real talent," and "A brash, confident young voice." I feel my erection grow stronger. Within seconds of reading blurbs about myself, I come. A lot. It goes everywhere: her ass, her back, her hair, the books.

"Wow," Suki says. "Where did that come from?"

"A really dark place," I say. And then I mope to the other side of the apartment to get a beer and check my e-mail. I'm not healthy.

University of Suck

As I toiled in the Hypermart family, Dora convinced me to enroll as an English student at the University of Winnipeg. She made a very strong case that a future as a writer may be attainable if I were to have some knowledge of literary tradition and contemporary practice. She was so smart about such things. I enrolled in a first-year creative writing class and unlocked my writer's chest for good. Now was the time to share the *A* material. After all, how else would I maintain an *A* average?

The teacher of the course was Carmen Adams — a very well-known local poet and publisher. She owned the most prestigious literary magazine in town. It was called *borderless,* and she was the kind of person who could make or break a young writer's career, even though she never seemed to acknowledge or cherish this power. She was a greying woman of about fifty-five, sharply dressed in a pin-striped charcoal suit. She looked perfect. She glared at me when I first stepped into her class — I was fifteen minutes late. I was dressed in an old Nirvana T-shirt, ripped vintage dress pants, and a jaunty Shill station ball cap.

"I'm sorry, but the small engine repair class is down the hall," she said. The class snickered.

"No. I'm here for writing . . . creative, like, writing."

"Well, with such a command of the English language,

I'm afraid there's not much I can teach you." More laughter. More embarrassment. "Take a seat, kid."

"It's Jonny."

"Yes, Jonny. Take a seat."

Our classes went from 8 P.M. until 10 P.M. on Mondays and Wednesdays. And then we would often continue our literary discussions at the King's Head Pub. Carmen would drink double Scotch on the rocks, smoke Pall Mall cigarettes, and hold court for hours talking about Gertrude Stein, T.S. Eliot, James Joyce, and Canadian writers too, like Alice Munro, Margaret Atwood, Leonard Cohen. She had a way of treating her students that was unlike any teacher I had encountered before. She could be gruff and cutting, but she was equally generous. And she did not treat any of us like students after that first class where she tried to scare the shit out of us (she confessed that her strategy was to try to frighten away students on the first day to make her marking loud lighter), she treated us like peers — like fellow writers. It was astonishing, and it was just what so many of us needed. Instead of keeping her knowledge about the publishing world to herself, she shared it openly. And those of us who wanted this knowledge listened attentively.

I hated Alec Bligh. He wore sweater vests and argyle ties. He tossed around Ezra Pound quotes like candy. And Carmen loved him and loved to joust with him. In the classroom, he would consistently bring up the concept of craft. His implied position was that poetry and literary fiction should follow a rigorous set of rules and requirements. If the writing didn't meet these requirements, it wasn't good writing. I was experimenting with riffing on the beat poets and Gertrude Stein, and attempting to create my very own kind of poem: the short-long poem — one that had the sensibilities and rhetoric of a classic long poem, yet was delivered in short bursts. It was meant to be the literary equivalent of the mullet. He was against experimentation and responded by hitting me over the head with excerpts from T.S. Eliot's "Tradition and the Individual Talent," and offering up his own very British-sounding sonnets and sestinas. After he attempted to tear apart my short-long poem, "Wheat Shafts," in front of the class, Carmen put him in his place.

First, for the sake of complete disclosure, here's the poem:

Wheat Shafts

wheat shafts
tall and long
like blossoming
penises under
watchful eye
of a fascist
grain elevator.
o shafts
you remind
me of my
father just before
his vasectomy

Alec called the poem "pure rubbish." I was, at the time, quite proud of my breakthrough, and sulked in my chair as he rambled on about what makes a good nature poem. Then Carmen saved me.

"Alec," she said, "why is it that your model for good literature is limited to such a small group of writers?"

"Because writing *is* a difficult game, Carmen," Alec said smugly. The entire class rolled their eyes simultaneously.

"Writing is difficult. But why do you think it's a game? Who do you think wins? Who loses?"

"Well. It's a turn of phrase."

"Yes, Alec. Congratulations on your skillful use of figurative language. But you understand that the library is quite large for a reason, and the canon is quite large for a reason."

"Because there are so many bad writers and so many people with bad taste. It's almost unbearable."

"You understand that if you had your way, literature would be reduced to a very rigid practice."

"Yes. There would be higher standards in my ideal world."

"And do you know what that would lead to?"

"Quality writing?"

"No, Alec. It would lead to row after row of identical artifacts. Each artifact would be so exquisitely crafted, so completely not unique. Your desire is to reduce the literary artist to the level of the artisan. And if you were to have this desire fulfilled, every poem would be an exercise in craft. And every poet would be Alec: a smug, white, young man of privilege, wearing a sweater vest and a necktie, and contemplating the emblematic resonance of a goddamned willow tree."

For the first time that year, Alec was quiet. And I was in awe of Carmen. At that moment, she was perfect.

But it turned out that Carmen Adams was not a perfect pedagogue. In fact, she had what some might consider a bit of a problem. She kept fucking her students: young men and young women who would turn to her for advice and guidance. She would mistake their adoration and respect for romantic love every time, and she would take them as lovers. I first discovered her propensity for getting it on with the kids when I walked in on her and Alec Bligh — the neo-formalist! — making out in the men's washroom of the King's Head. They were both flustered at getting busted so I just winked at them in order to ease the situation. I couldn't believe it though. That arrogant prick was shoving his British tongue down my favourite teacher's throat.

Carmen had made one very good decision that year. She hired me to run the affairs of her literary magazine. I was her managing editor. I think she hired me in part because I knew nothing of finances or business practices, and she didn't particularly need some nosy, fiscally responsible student looking too closely into her affairs. I also think she hired me in part because I wanted it so bad. I wanted to learn how the publication and dissemination of literature worked. I wanted to work it. Dora told me to go after it, and I had taken that to heart.

Three years of my undergraduate career were spent in Carmen's office, slowly trudging my way toward an acceptable comprehension of the literary world. When I wasn't bookkeeping or line-editing, I was lost in one of her books: Will Self, Gilbert Sorrentino, Gertrude Stein, Lyn Hejinian.

One day, as we pored over unsolicited submissions, I mustered the courage to ask her something that had been on my mind from the first time I had seen her snogging that neo-formalist poetaster undergrad.

"Hey, Carmen?"

"Yeah, Jonny?"

"How come we never fooled around?"

She laughed. "I don't know. You're not my type I guess."

"You mean sycophantic?"

"That's evil, Jonny. You have an evil streak. It's very pleasant."

"So why not for real?"

"It's hard to say. I know I'm weak. All of the lovers I have had in my life recently have been young, needy people. But even compared to them, your needs are too much. You are too needy, Jonny. And that's a compliment."

"How is that in any way a compliment?"

"I'll try to explain." She leaned back in her chair and posed regally for a moment, before leaning in and making intense eye contact. She was very good at using her teaching tricks outside of the teaching context. "Do you remember, as a child, maybe you were walking to the playground, or maybe you were at the playground, or in a backyard, or a neighbour's backyard . . ."

"Okay. Sure . . ."

"And do you remember that maybe things all of a sudden seemed unreal for the first time? Like, for the first time in your life you realized that you were a subject, and you were alone, and you were impermanent?"

"Yeah. . . . Yeah! I totally do. I was very young. Too young. I was crawling on shag carpet. And there was Johnny Carson, and my grandfather, and polyester, and all of a sudden, the world seemed to tilt and I realized I would remember that feeling forever. And I would remember that I was alone. And yet, not alone."

"Right. You were all alone. Completely alone. But you discovered some company: something tactile and beautiful, and you discovered perception, and the harsh yet comforting feeling of the shag carpet, and I bet your grandfather was laughing, and you were laughing, and it was at once warm and disturbing."

"Well, something like that."

"Do you know what that's about?"

"Immortality?"

"Imagery, Jonny. Specifically, it's about writing. That's about your subjectivity. It's the gift you bring to writing. You see, Jonny. The thing that most people don't understand is that writing is not about being sophisticated. Writing is not about being an adult. Writing is about being a child."

"I don't understand."

"Being a child is about losing yourself in imagination and play. Being an adult is about losing yourself to your lack of imagination and your inability to play. Writing is an ongoing attempt to get back to that first moment where you realize that things aren't real and it's the most real thing you've ever experienced."

"So writers should endeavor to be childish?"

"No. The good writers already are, in a sense. And Jonny, you are one of the most childish people I've ever known."

I smiled. "Thanks."

I didn't realize at the time that she was fucking with me. It may be true that creative people are often childlike. But being childish did not guarantee that one would necessarily create, or create something artful. Carmen had a knack for tricking me. Or I had a knack for being tricked.

In the third year of my undergraduate career, she came round the office less and less. She was on a half-year sick leave. But she wouldn't tell me what exactly was wrong. She just said she needed some treatment, and she would be back to drinking and smoking in no time. Once again I was tricked into believing her. The last time I saw her, she was frail and almost lifeless. Her breaths were laboured and she moaned. She didn't want anyone to see her like that, especially those of us who selfishly needed her to be that strong, perfect woman who could guide us, and make us feel smarter and more hopeful than we ever deserved to be. But her extended family knew how close we had been and let me visit. I needed to at least say goodbye and thank you. She looked at me with kind eyes, but she couldn't speak. I wasn't sure if she was happy to see me or not, but I just sat there and provided her with all the literary gossip of the past year. She acknowledged me at one point with a very subtle smile — I was sure of it — when I complained that Alec Bligh had received a national grant to complete his first book of poems, *The Thinking Tree of Thought.*

I wish I could deliver some sort of punchline at this point, but there's nothing funny about this. And there's no big lesson to this either, no moral, nothing to be gleaned. Carmen deserved to be around longer, to be a bigger part of my life — to be a better and more developed character in this book. There is no other way to say it. It just sucks.

Mystery Shopped!

I have a theory: when God had completed his designs of the greatest douche bags of humanity, he wasn't entirely pleased. Oh sure, he had prototypes for the lawyer, the bureaucrat, the world leader, but God felt there was something missing: an ultimate douche who could self-righteously ruin people's lives under a cloak of anonymity and retail prowess. This überdouche was dubbed the mystery shopper. The mystery shopper's job would be to pretend to buy products from various retail stores and use this cover to evaluate how obedient the poor, minimum-wage-making employees were to the companies who oppressed them.

God was particularly proud of the mystery shopper. Of all the men and women he had created, this model was the closest to his own image. My own encounter with a mystery shopper affirms this theory. And I will get to that in a moment, but first I must assert that my theory is stupid because there is no God. I have proof.

There was a time I almost believed in God. My parents had become even more zealous about their respective personal relationships with the Lord, Jesus. They would drag me to the Transcona Revival Church every Sunday morning for the quakingest, shakingest, tongues-speakingest church service in all of Winnipeg. My brother would stay home in protest, listen to Black Sabbath, and threaten to drink goat's blood. I was with him in defiant spirit, but at the age of fourteen, I was still not quite old enough to stand up to the wrath of God and my parents. My parents had become leaders in the church, and they would burst into a blue streak of holy nonsense on a weekly basis.

"Mwwhajibiiti liminihinina abitabbi abitabbi!" my mom would scream.

"Allawai allawai shaddai shaddai dibrinititi!" my dad would respond.

And other members of the congregation would pop out of their seats, as if they were victims of divine puppetry, and start adding their voices to the gibberish choir. The pastor would sway, his beard glistening with sweat, or the oil of anointment, or whatever, the people would sway and get all trippy, and I would remain seated, my face flush with embarrassment.

One Sunday, however, I caught a glimpse of something divine in that church filled with charlatans and suckwads. Her name was Chastity Neufeld. She too had the gift of tongues, and at the tender age of fifteen! But when she spoke the holy language of God, she heaved and sashayed, she gyrated and groaned. And her voice was soft and sensual as if she were some actress from a dubbed French erotic movie that you might be lucky enough to glimpse on late-night CBC.

When I first saw her I sprung from my seat. My father looked at me with anticipation. Perhaps I was about to emote in God's own dialect! But no. I just stood there, my eyes lost in that swaying, super-developed body, that angelic face, those endless freckles, that light red hair.

For weeks, I would pick my spot and stand at attention, taking in all the glory of Chastity Neufeld. I would attempt to get her attention with a knowing smile, or an intense, arousing stare. But nothing seemed to divert her attention from Jesus and those who appeared to communicate directly with Jesus. Finally, one Sunday, I devised a plan to get her attention. I would give the performance of my life and speak in tongues with such a convincingly authentic tone that I would impress everyone. I would be the golden child, and Chastity would be my child bride. The strange thing is, and I don't know quite how to express this, but the closer I came to affecting some sort of public relationship with God, the closer and closer I became to actually believing. Rationally, I knew that I was hatching a plan to fake-communicate with God, but the more emotionally invested I became in the plan and the more I envisioned its best possible outcome (me and sweet Chastity dry humping in the back of her father's station wagon), the more it seemed possible that God was real and there was a purpose.

The night before I was to unleash my plan on an unsuspecting congregation, I said a little prayer:

Dear Jesus H. Christ,

If you actually exist and are actually the son of God, and if you can hear this, please don't take offense at what I'm gonna do. I'm not trying to make fun of you or your dad. I just want to impress a girl. You must know the feeling. I mean . . . I know you preferred dudes when you roamed this earth. I mean . . . you had like twelve boyfriends right? Where I come from that's totally being a man whore. No offense again. You must know what it's like to want something so bad that you can feel it in your pants, or your robe, or whatever. Anyways. I want this girl really bad. She is the only good thing about church. Jesus! No offense. Shit, I mean, sorry. But listen, guy, if you can see it in your heart, please let tomorrow go well for me. If you make her love me, I will totally kill my brother for you.

Your servant,
Jonny

The church was a feverish frenzy of hand waving, progressive Christian rock, and tongues when Chastity began her chanting.

"Zallawa Mennahah! Zallawa Mennahah! Shaddani! Shaddani Mennanah!" she cooed.

I took my cue, jumped up and emoted. But what came out sounded less holy and exactly like David Lee Roth scatting in "Just a Gigolo": "Hummala beeboola zimmila bop! Boze-dy boze-dy bop! Zee bop! Zee bop!" I don't know why that came out. I guess I choked. The entire church was looking at me. Some looked at me with disdain in their eyes, others were simply confused. But they were all looking. I tried again but it just got more unfortunate: "Calrissian! Calrissian! Chewbacca Yoda! Chewbacca Yoda!"

And before I could even look over at Chastity Neufeld, I was grabbed by the scruff of the neck and escorted out of the worship area by a burly usher. In the pastor's office, I sat facing my mom and dad and Pastor Dave. Mom was sobbing a little and Dad looked like he was ready to not spare the rod. Pastor Dave spoke.

"Jonny, what the heck were you doing out there? I mean, gosh, Jonny, that little display was just so inappropriate."

"I felt the spirit of God speaking through me, Pastor Dave."

I heard my dad whisper, "Help me, Jesus," under his breath.

"Okay, Jonny. I think I understand," said the pastor.

"You do?"

"Yes. Jonny, you have what we in the ministry call a 'false gift.' You see, when you are given the gift of tongues, it's clear to everyone else who has it that it is authentic. Your words today were not from the Lord. They were from the enemy."

"What the fuck?"

"See, that's Satan speaking through you right now!"

"Jesus Christ! This is fucked."

Then Pastor Dave lunged at me, over his desk, tackling me and holding me down on his office floor. His sweaty palm mashed up against my face and his hairy, chubby body rubbed up against mine as he had me pinned. He began to chant: "I rebuke you, vile spirit! In the name of Jesus, our lord and saviour, I rebuke you. Leave this child! Leave this child at once!" He began grinding up against me and I could feel his erection under his purple robe.

"Oh God! Will he be okay?" Mom asked.

"Give me a minute," Pastor Dave said as he continued shaking my head and rubbing himself against my thigh. I wrestled my way out of his death grip and retreated to the far corner of the room, shaking and curled up like a frightened, feral cat. "The spirit is gone," Pastor Dave said.

"Praise God!" Dad said.

I said nothing. My parents were told to keep me away from the church for a couple of weeks. A kind of probation. I swore to myself that I would take the opportunity to learn more from my brother about Satan.

The next time I saw Chastity Neufeld was at Hypermart. She had put on some weight, but she still looked incredible. She chose my till to purchase her Hypermart brand diet cream soda and her Hypermart brand double-pack of cheese-flavoured "snack rods." She looked at me with kindness and understanding. It was like we had been to war together, or waged spiritual warfare together, or something.

"You're that kid who was possessed, eh?"

"Yeah, well. I wasn't really. I was actually trying to get your attention."

"Really? That's kind of retarded."

I passed her merchandise over the scanner, as I tried to give her a sexy, squinty, "all-grown-up" kinda look. "Yeah. Fair enough. But I was a kid. And I had a huge crush on you. As you can plainly see, I am a man now. A grown man. A man with a job and even a place to live."

"Well, congratulations on all your success."

"So umm. Do you still like God?"

She rolled her eyes. "Yes. I am still a servant of the Lord."

"Oh. That's cool. I mean, Jesus is alright. He's no Travis Bickle, but he's, like, pretty cool. I mean, he changed the way we think about umm . . . carpentry and man love."

"Whatever."

"Listen, I kind of have a girlfriend. Her name is Dora. But if you ever wanna like fuck around, or do some drugs, or something, I could, like, give you my number. If she answers, just hang up, but if I answer we could make plans and, you know, maybe screw sometime."

"Wow. Yeah . . . No. That's disgusting. You're disgusting."

I scrawled my number on her receipt. "Well, I tend to grow on people. You know, like fungus, or yeast. I mean, you might see me tonight in your dreams, whether you want to or not."

She said nothing. She just shuddered, grabbed her bag and scurried off. I called out after her. "Have a hyper day!" And then she was gone.

A week later, Mr. Hardman called me into his office and showed me this:

HYPERMART MYSTERY SHOPPER REPORT #2942

Cashier: Jonny.

Store: 157

Did employee express a warm and friendly Hypermart greeting?
No.

Did employee ask if you had a Hypermart credit card?
No.

Did employee mention the Hypermart points promotion?
No.

Did employee mention any pertinent cross promotions?
No.

Was employee helpful?
No.

Was employee polite?
No.

Did employee display signs of functional intelligence?
No.

Was employee well-groomed?
No.

Did employee have his shirt tucked in?
No.

Did employee wish you "a hyper day"?
Yes.

Additional notes:
This cashier was extremely rude and asked to have sexual intercourse with me and/or to abuse drugs. He gave me his phone number, and I felt personally threatened by his insistence. He told me I would have dreams of him, and that he would grow on me "like a fungus."

Final mark:
10%

Recommendation:
Immediate dismissal.

At first I wasn't sure who the mystery shopper was, because I tended to make such offers frequently, but the "like a fungus" line was the tip-off. I save my *A* material for people I truly care about.

"So, Jonny? What do you have to say for yourself?" Mr. Hardman asked.

"Oh shit, Mr. Hardman. I know who this mystery shopper is! This is a setup! I can prove it!"

"Yeah?"

"Yeah, Mr. Hardman. I would bet my life that this mystery shopper is a young woman, around my age, and her name is Chastity."

Hardman paused. "How did you know that?"

"Well, she was my first love. And I broke her heart. Like seriously broke the fuck out of it! You know, Mr. Hardman, I'm like Captain Kirk when he beams down to some planet and starts making out with a hot alien lady, and the alien lady is all 'Why are you pressing your lips against mine?' And Captain Kirk is all, 'It's a custom from Earth.' And the alien lady says, 'Please, custom me again.' I'm like that. So anyways, we were dating and she got all clingy, and you know me, I like to ramble and stuff, so it wasn't a match for me. I had to cut her loose. Now she's trying to exact revenge! Don't let her jilted heart ruin my Hypermart career, Mr. Hardman!"

Mr. Hardman was silent. Then after a few tumbleweed moments, I was told to stay away from Hypermart for a couple of weeks. A kind of unpaid probation. I swore to myself that I would take the opportunity to hunt Chastity down and ruin her life, unless she called me and wanted to screw around or something.

I had always wanted to fit in — everywhere, with everyone, in every situation. But Hypermart changed things. I was simply too disgusted with what had happened to my strip mall, and to my life. It was like I had been demoted from person to Hypermart employee. I had never done a great job in any capacity, but I worked extra hard to be the ultimate slacker when it came to my Hypermart duties. I know this resulted in a string of horrible evaluations, and conclusions about my intelligence or sanity. But I discovered something by having to listen to these constant claims that I would never succeed. It turned out that I did possess one very important quality: defiance. Whenever faced with the cruel judgments of people like Chastity Neufeld or Mr. Hardman, I would remember the following mantra: *I do not want to thrive in YOUR world.*

The Hostility Suite

I wrote what I knew. I wrote for myself. I wrote for Carmen. I wrote for my grandfather, the notion of polyester. The result was a book of semi-autobiographical comedy called *Asthmatronics.* It got me into book festivals. It got me on the radio and even TV. It got me writing about myself, and writing about writing about myself. I was spiralling. Here's a radio essay I wrote around the time of my B-level emergence:

Red Cosmopolis Literary Festival, Montreal, QC.
Stardate: 2005.6

I had nothing to do but enjoy Red Cosmopolis this year. Last year, I was all over the panels, performing my not-so-famous prairie angst poetry, hiding from imaginary groupies, and signing autographs for my mom — it was exhausting. But this year, I was all about my own literary enlightenment. I was determined to see all that I could see, learn all I could learn, and possibly meet some famous writers in the process. This was Jonny's year to kick back and relax.

The first thing that struck me, in the lobby of the Hyatt Regency, was how Red Cosmopolis resembles a *Star Trek* convention. Sure, there may be an absence of Spock ears and Seven-of-Nine lip gloss, but there were just the right number of weird old men in philosopher beards and moping celibates with plastic-rimmed glasses to make me feel right at home.

Now this may seem hard to believe, but I haven't quite been able to make a living off *Asthmatronics*. This is particularly depressing considering Jackson had recently spoken his first word, and it was "royalties." So, I had to find a way to get free tickets.

With a half-drunk bottle of Zima, I bribed a CBC radio producer into telling me where the Hostility Suite was. Room 226. Perfect. The "Hostility Suite" is writer code for the "Hospitality Suite," the hotel room where all the authors and important media types congregate to enjoy free wine, beer, and saltines. Hostility Suite — it's the kind of delicious wordplay that could only come from a highly sophisticated literary mind. (Legend has it that T.S. Eliot first coined the term while kibitzing with Ezra Pound at the 1933 Hartford Poetry Rodeo.) My idea was to get up to the suite, apply some of my sweet Jonny charm on some unsuspecting writers, and get on some guest lists.

When I arrived at the suite, it wasn't "Writers Gone Wild" as I remembered it from last year. This year, it was all Dolce this and Gabbana that, Botox this and Kaballah that, Smokey this and the Bandit that. Suddenly the festival seemed upwardly mobile. I quickly realized that I was outclassed by this year's crop of talent. Still, I boldly entered the room and flashed my pearly whites. Hello, Fellow Writers! Who wants to hear a harrowing tale of prairie frostbite?

Elliot Clarke Francis was sipping on complimentary Merlot, and dishing with Jose Fuentes: "Did you see that ensemble Michael Chudley wore at Harbourfront? It's like, 1992 called, and it wants its mock turtleneck back! And WHAT is with that hair?" Elliot said.

"Yes, indeed. Who does he think he is? Geddy Lee?" Jose offered. I was struck by how much Mr. Fuentes looked like Victor from *Days of Our Lives*, and I got momentarily lost in a daydream in which Mr. Fuentes slapped me across the face and exclaimed, "You're not my son, you bastard! I . . . have . . . no . . . son."

Some of the local authors had torn down the no smoking signs and were lighting up left and right. These were the "bad boys" of the festival — my people! Despite the imminent asthma attack I would suffer for staying in the smoky fray, I schmoozed my way to the hipsters, and tried to find a kindred spirit. Local performance poet, Da Kid, was holding court, regaling her fellow scribes with a tall tale about a certain kind of hamster that resembles the human kidney. Local cartoonist and lecherous dude, Billy Thessilonikas, had brought fishcakes for all, and was dispensing them liberally. My optimism was quickly curbed, however, as the party banter devolved to a simple bitchiness:

"I noticed Munro finally got the work done," said one scribe.

"Yeah, what took her so long? It's not as if those jowls were gonna lift themselves!" added another.

I wondered if the 1933 Hartford Poetry Rodeo suffered from similar gossip like: "I can't believe Gertrude Stein is wearing the same seafoam green bustle dress as Marianne Moore! It's on now, sister!" Also I wondered where the debauchery was. I seemed to remember that in past years at Red Cos, the Hostility Suite was the site of countless rounds of drinking games, belching contests, pantsless knife fights. I recalled beer bongs! This was the Red Cos experience I remembered. Had everyone grown up but me?

As the evening went on, there was talk of agents, and whose agent dumped whom, and whose ghost writer was found where doing what with whose agent, and so on. I decided that if I was to get on anyone's good side and guest list, I was going to have to say something. I was going to have to come up with a clever quip. I set my sights on a group of young local writers.

"Hey guys, what's the deal with that Tito Puente guy? Why is he here? Didn't he, like, write that 'Mambo #5' song? That song sucks! Am I right or what?" I said.

Dead silence. Behind me, I glimpsed Jose Fuentes, with a huge Cuban cigar in his mouth. "Not funny, dude," he said, and he put his index finger over my lips as if to shush me, then ashed his cigar in my hair. That was SOOOO Victor of him. I sulked back into the shadows and tried to put myself together. I began to think that my place was probably with the people — the weird bearded dudes, the sulking celibates, the aspiring writers. Yet, for some reason, I stayed in the Hostility Suite and did my best damage control, mingling and feigning interest the whole night through.

When I was a boy, my synchronized swimming coach used to tell me that I had the heart of an Olympian but unfortunately, the brain of a Special Olympian. It's true that I'm not all that smart of a guy. Some have remarked that I'm as thick as Leonard Cohen's back hair. But I did learn some things in the Hostility Suite. Things like: a pussy willow swaying in the breeze is a good poetic image to represent the human condition; you should never wear Gucci at a book launch these days — it's simply gauche; and most important, wearing a cardigan and saying phrases like, "Hi, I can get you published, and I'm in Room 1403" can get you quite far. By the time these lessons were learned, however, I had missed all of the events I wanted to see, including the "Mitsou for Nobel Laureate" panel. In the end, I guess my Red Cos experience was full of life lessons. But I often find that by the time I am ready to apply these lessons, the right moments have passed. I suppose it's like that old Jose Fuentes saying: "Like sand through the hourglass, so are the days of our lives."

Jonny's Mid-life Crisis Report: Entry #9

There is a story to be told. A story about a young man who needs to write and the strip mall he calls home. And I was at a loss. I didn't know how to seal the deal until now. Evan has introduced me to the world of narrative art. He has also reintroduced me to cocaine, Norman Rockwell, and man-on-man action. I'm mildly concerned about the repercussions of two of these three things.

Evan pulls me into his world and challenges me. He makes me read comic books. Not *Archie* comic books, but graphic novels: *V for Vendetta, Ghost World, American Splendor, Louis Riel, My Most Secret Desire, Blue Monday, Jimmy Corrigan.* I think about the strip mall; I think about its imagery, its absurd beauty; its fatal archaic neon and handmade signs, its flickering lamplight, the hopeless, helpless teenagers who haunted it and haunted me. I think about how much of this is actually fictional. And I turn to Evan, offer him my world of words, and, in turn, I ask him to offer me a visual world. A strip mall world.

It is 11 A.M. on a Friday night. I have been working feverishly for days. Working so hard that I completely forgot to drink for the last two days. I have, however, been smoking like Tom Snyder before Lent. I think it's affecting me. My cultural references are disturbingly anachronistic. I trudge through the snow from St. Urbain, down Esplanade to Mont-Royal, and finally to Parc Avenue and Evan's front door. I can hear "Time Is on My Side" by the Rolling Stones and smell cinnamon incense. I peek in his front window and I see two silhouettes. One is the slender Evan, and the other is an even more slender young woman. They are lip-locked and my heart sags, but just a little. I fold up my script and slide it through his mail slot, along with a simple note:

Dear Evan,

I hope you can do something with this.

Love,
Jonny

Stripmalling

A COMIC BOOK BY JONNY AND EVAN

I WAS BORN HERE. IN THIS STRIP MALL.

WELL, NOT REALLY, BUT IT SEEMED LIKE A GOOD WAY TO BEGIN A STORY.

I LIVE HERE THOUGH, IN THIS STRIP MALL, IN MY CHEVETTE, BEHIND THE SHELL STATION. IT'S WAY CHEAPER THAN PAYING RENT, AND BEING A GAS JOCKEY ISN'T VERY LUCRATIVE.

I GET PAID IN CASH.

IT'S 7 A.M. TIME TO OPEN THE STATION.

I'M ON THE MORNING SHIFT AS A PUNISHMENT FOR HOT BOXING THE STATION LAST WEEK WITH MY FRIEND SANDY SEV. SHE WORKS AT THE SEV.

THE STRIP MALL WORLD IS A WORLD OF CONTRADICTIONS. IT'S A RETAIL CULTURE BUT IT'S UNDERGROUND CULTURE TOO.

IT'S DRUG DEALERS AND DROP-IN CENTRES. IT'S GIRLFRIENDS AND TYRANT BOSSES . . .

. . . THERE'S A LARGE SIGN IN THE WINDOW OF THE SHELL STATION THAT SAYS **NO LOITERING**. BUT THAT'S ALL ANY OF US REALLY DO HERE . . .

NO LOITERING

113

BESIDES, SHE VOLUNTEERS AT THE DROP-IN CENTRE AND SHE WANTS TO FOCUS ON HELPING AT-RISK YOUTH.

I KNOW SANDY SEV USED TO CUT HER COKE WITH BABY FORMULA TOO. IT'S ONE OF THE TRICKS OF THE TRADE.

IT'S KIND OF NECESSARY IF YOU WANT TO MAKE A PROFIT.

AND BESIDES, THERE'S NOTHING UNHEALTHY ABOUT BABY FORMULA. I'M GIVING THESE KIDS SOME MUCH-NEEDED VITAMINS AND NUTRIENTS.

119

AS YOU MAY HAVE GUESSED, STORE 157 DIDN'T LAST ANOTHER FISCAL YEAR.

HYPERMART LEFT AN EMPTY BOX-SHAPED TOMB IN OUR OLD STRIP MALL AND EAST TRANSCONA WAS A GHOST TOWN.

JONNY AND I WERE ON TO BIGGER AND BETTER THINGS. I HAD BEEN ACCEPTED TO MCGILL FOR DOCTORAL STUDIES IN DEVELOPMENTAL PSYCHOLOGY.

AND JONNY WAS GROWING MORE CONFIDENT BY THE DAY. HE KNEW THAT HE WAS GOING TO BE A WRITER. A GOOD ONE. AND I WAS MORE THAN WILLING TO HELP HIM.

I BELIEVED IN JONNY.

125

The Dora Report: Entry #4

I think I'm over Jonny. I met someone who is talented and sensitive. He is kind and selfless. He has a drug problem, but no one's perfect. We met at a bar on Parc Avenue. We shot pool and he made me laugh. It's pretty hard to make me laugh. He seems to have perfect instincts when it comes to me. Great anticipation. Great kisser. I wonder if I should introduce him to Jackson. In due time, I suppose, if he's not a fuck-up. He is an artist. A painter and illustrator. He's not successful yet, but he will be. That kind of scares me. When Jonny got just a little taste of success with his writing, his priorities shifted. At some point he stopped being Jonny, and became a character named Jonny in one of his stupid stories.

But not everyone reduces himself or herself to a pat character. I should have faith that not everyone is as hard-wired for self-injury as Jonny is. So, I think I will be cautious. But it does feel good to be wanted, desired, appreciated. I think he's falling hard. He is always sketching me. I would like to put my faith in Evan.

Jonny's Mid-life Crisis Report: Final Entry

I call Dora; it's 3 A.M. One year to the day I left her. I have a tendency to do this sort of thing for trivial reasons. But this time it's more meaningful than I can express. I feel I have come through my self-injurious year; I've sold my book, and although I'm sufficiently injured, I am somehow stronger. Myself again. I don't drink very much; I don't sweat profusely after walking up one flight of stairs. . . . The gamble was always this: would she still be home when I was ready to come home?

No answer.

I call again. She answers with a half-groan, half-whisper, "Hello?"

"Say something lovely."

Instructions for Soliciting Forgiveness

For this project you will need the following:

One fortune cookie (in wrapper).
One set of tweezers.
One pair of scissors.
One sheet of blank paper.
A fine-tip red marker.
Non-toxic glue.

Step one: Take the fortune cookie out of its wrapper.
Step two: Take tweezers and remove the fortune.
Step three: Cut a fortune-sized piece of paper.
Step four: Take your fine-tip marker and write:
I'm sorry.
Step five: Put the paper in the fortune cookie.
Step six: Put the fortune cookie in the wrapper.
Step seven: Glue the wrapper shut.
Step eight: Leave fortune cookie in Dora's mailbox.
Step nine: Run like hell.

David Letterman, Hardwood, and Polyester

Jackson is on the unfinished hardwood floor, playing with his Barbies. Truly his father's son. In the stand-up kitchen, boxes of empties are piled up in the corner; bills are piled up on the fridge. Across the room is my desk. A stack of paper containing the latest manuscript version of *Stripmalling* is placed neatly beside my laptop. Some order amid the chaos.

I am on the futon that doubles as my bed. My cheap Value Village "professor" blazer is splayed on the floor like a polyester rug. I crack open a diet soda. Soon I will have to inflate Jackson's air mattress, and read to him until he falls asleep. Right now we are almost halfway through *Of Grammatology*. So far, Jackson's a bit suspicious of post-structuralism.

For now, Letterman's on and he's doing one of his bits: "Is This Anything?" It's not classic comedy. It's like meta-comedy. They simply open the curtain and there's some weird dude juggling knives, dancing girls, Hula-Hoop girls, and maybe a contortionist, and Dave and Paul debate as to whether or not it is anything. For some reason it always makes me laugh.

Jackson looks up at me and laughs too.

Bonus Material

The Jonny and Dora Interview

Dora: So, let's begin.

Jonny: Thanks for having me.

Dora: Whatever. You asked me to do this.

Jonny: Can you just stay in character for Chrissakes?

Dora: I would suggest that it's you who is out of character. You used to be a sweet guy: dedicated, kind, obedient. I mean sure, you ripped off skater kids with bad drugs and stole from the Shill station. But you used to have a good heart.

Jonny: Did you really just say "obedient"?

Dora: Well, you were.

Jonny: Well, that's a problem isn't it? Maybe I needed to stop taking orders and find myself.

Dora: That's a cliché if I ever heard one. "Find yourself." And how do you find yourself now?

Jonny: Pretty sad. I drink too much.

Dora: Why?

Jonny: Because it's in my blood. My family is a long line of drinkers. My mom and dad lost the plot. But I am restoring the narrative.

Dora: You're horrible at narrative.

Jonny: I know. That's why you're here.

Dora: So you're using me.

Jonny: Yes.

Dora: Why did you leave me?

Jonny: I was scared of my bad behaviour. It was hurting you. I don't want to hurt you.

Dora: Bullshit.

Jonny: Okay. Here's the thing. I needed to renew my dedication to writing and to my craft, and that involved staying true to the tradition that Carmen established, and the hopes and dreams of my grandfather.

Dora: Holy shit, Jonny. That's a cop-out. Don't claim some

sort of nobility out of this. The truth is that the very moderate success you had gave you a taste for sycophancy, and you liked it.

Jonny: What the hell are you talking about?

Dora: The only people who hang out with you, who will sleep with you, who show interest in you, are actually just showing interest in themselves. They want to publish, or to have some sort of credibility in your writerly world. It's sick, Jonny. And it's sick that you chose that over something real.

Jonny: That's no way to talk about yourself.

Dora: What?

Jonny: Well, you still show interest in me. So you must want to get published then.

Dora: That's different.

Jonny: How? Are you the only one capable of caring for me in a genuine way?

Dora: Probably.

Jonny: Right.

Dora: And the sad thing is that you've become a performance that resembles your former self. The self-defined loser, beta male. It's pleasant at first, but you should be capable of more.

Jonny: And you should be capable of compassion. Listen. I may not have much to offer. But at least I offer it.

Dora: What does that evan mean?

Jonny: Did you just say, "What does that EVAN mean?" Jesus, Dora! This is all so gross. It means that I don't protect myself from being happy. Also it just sounds good.

Dora: Did you know that Jackson has taken a huge step forward in perspective taking?

Jonny: Not now, Dora. Tell me about it off the record.

Dora: Wait. It's important. He said to me: "Even though Bootsy thinks she's a good cat, she actually isn't."

Jonny: Cute.

Dora: And I couldn't resist. I asked Jackson about you.

Jonny: And?

Dora: He said: "Daddy's alright. He's a bit of a douche."

Jonny: That's amazing!

Dora: Why, Jonny? Why is it amazing? Because it's subject matter? Because it's kind of funny? That's what this is all about. It's sick. You tell me you are trying to write your way out of a crisis, but really, you are just using the people who love you. You've reduced us to characters in one of your fucking little books. It's so gross.

Jonny: Hold on. You're the hero of this book, and Jackson is portrayed with a very, um, thoughtful pen.

Dora: What does that even mean? We are characters. Sloppily written characters in yet another unfunny "comedic romp" by Jonny. You know what the sad thing is? Like, the really tragic thing? You think that you are embedding some sort of political message about the idea of corporate giants, and big-box stores ruining real people's lives and communities. And maybe you actually get that point across. Maybe you actually succeed in saying something for once. But on an interpersonal level, you are doing exactly what those stores did to the strip mall.

Jonny: Huh?

Company Pamphlets

JOIN THE HYPERMART FAMILY!

LOOK HOW HUGE IT IS!

In 1973, Slim Wilton founded Hypermart Inc. with three guiding principles: value the dollar, service our customers, and strive to ruin small towns and communities across North America by establishing a monolithic retail force that destroys small business and local culture. Needless to say, it was a really awesome formula for success. Hypermart has grown into the largest retail business on Earth. And you must submit to it. You simply must. In 2003, *$weet* magazine recognized Hypermart as one of the world's "Most Fucking Scary Companies." Over the years, Hypermart has received great honours from the top business publications and associations. Last year, Satan himself presented Slim Wilton with a lifetime achievement award in the field of Douche Baggery.

IT'S ALL ABOUT THE BIPEDS!

Hypermart is one of the fastest growing and least equitable employers in the world! We offer unlimited opportunities for people of all ages who are interested in retailing and stagnation. From computer guy to sculptor, store manager to cashier, it can all be done at Hypermart. Young or old, black or white, or some other colour, Hypermart has a way to exploit the little life you have left. If you can walk, you are Hypermart material! Apply today at your local Hypermart! Just look out the window. We're there!

DO YOU HAVE WHAT IT TAKES TO MAKE THE SHILL TEAM??

THE FUTURE IS GASEOUS!
Shill Canada is one of the few large players in the petroleum refining, marketing and retailing industry in North America. Shill is 100 percent owned by The Shill Petroleum Company Ltd. of Scotland, which is owned by the dual listed companies Awesome Oil of the Cayman Islands and Greasy Inc. of Muncie, Indiana.

Shill generated over $20.2 billion in revenue and recorded a net profit after tax of $291 million as at 31 December 2005. The company has assets worth more than $6.2 billion, and total employee count exceeded 8900 at the end of 2005. The company is involved in the exploration and production of crude oil and natural gas, as well as the manufacture and marketing of petroleum and chemical products. Which is great for everyone who cares about gas.

Shill has over 1000 Shill sites across North America selling fuel, lubricants, car care and convenience goods, and food on the run. As of 28 May 2003, following a deal struck with Shill and Supercentre Plus, the supermarket retailer who specializes in oil-based edible products such as coffee cream, various fruit-flavoured snacks, and delicious sandwiches, we will expand even further.

PUMP YOUR WAY TO THE TOP!

Shill is interested in finding open-minded individuals who would like to pump our gas into cars of various makes and models. If you enjoy sticking long nozzles into things, you have a future with us! Shill guarantees that it will comply with provincial- or state-determined minimum-wage legislation, and is committed to the wellness and development of its employees through its Shill Re-education Camps. Shill's passion is oil and people. Shill is proud of its ability to immerse people in oil.

Workshopped!

STRIPMALLING || *Find a better title*

by Jonny

Submitted to the downtown Montreal YMCA creative writing class, 2008.

(sp) Exit?   *— as in nudity?*

(EXT.) Regent Park (Strip) Mall — Wide shot. (Like a crane shot)   *bird or machine?*

nevermind! oops!

JONNY

I was born here. In this strip mall. Well, not really, but it seemed like a good way to begin a story. *it's not.*

EXT. Grey Chevette behind Shill Station — from behind and slightly above.

I live here though, in this strip mall, in my Chevette, behind the Shill Station. It's way cheaper than paying rent, and being a gas jockey isn't very lucrative. I get paid in cash. *?*

INT. Chevette passenger seat.   *impossible! (and illegal!)*

JONNY is smoking hash out of the cigarette lighter. Wearing a Ramones shirt, but looking young, fauxhawk, *?* fairly thin, and world-weary. | *fragment*

142

JONNY

is this a sex thing?

It's 7 a.m. Time to open the station. I'm on the morning
shift as a punishment for hot boxing the station last week
with my friend, Sandy Sev. She works at the Sev.

family name?

EXT. Front of Shill station. JONNY slips Shill coveralls
over his clothes unlocks the front door.

How so.

JONNY

The strip mall world is a world of contradictions. It's a
retail culture but it's underground culture too. It's drug
dealers and drop-in centres. It's girlfriends
and tyrant bosses... *oh. ok.*

EXT. Shadow of Jonny counting smokes inside, focus on
NO LOITERING SIGN outside.

. . There's a large sign in the window of the
Shill station that says NO LOITERING. But that's
all any of us really do here. . . .

INT. Night. Shill Station. Jonny is on the phone, ignoring
customers.

*literally? or is he
SPEAKING on the phone??
be clear!*

JONNY

I work a lot of double shifts. 7 a.m. to 3 p.m.
and then 3 p.m. till midnight I'm trying to save up my

fragment.

143

money for university tuition. I'm gonna [going to] be a writer.
I already have my muse.

I am in love with Dora. [WHO IS THIS??]

INT. Night. Libby's Discount Fabrics. Dora is on the phone, ignoring customers.

We make each other better people. Like Charles Grodin and Robert De Niro. I'm the Charles Grodin. And she is Robert De Niro . . . but with a vagina. [but men don't have vaginas!]

EXT. Night. Strip mall parking lot.

Dora and Jonny are sitting on the hood of his Chevette, smoking cigarettes and staring up at the sky. [as opposed to staring DOWN at the sky? come on!]

JONNY

One day, I will marry her . . .

Dora and Jonny still on the hood, now holding each other.

I'm gonna need a real apartment and some semblance of a future. Dora is the only person who knows I want to be a writer. Well, she's not the only one who knows. She's the only one who thinks it's a good idea. [we know too!]

EXT. Night. Strip mall parking lot. Jonny is dealing weed
to two skater kids out of his car.

JONNY [previously established]

I'm a bit of a douche. Dora knows this.
I sell drugs to the kids from the drop-in centre. But I am
saving up for college so it's not all that bad.

SKATER KID #1 (Dialogue)

Hey, Jonny, when are you gonna get some more blow? [blow what??]

JONNY (Dialogue)

Probably tomorrow night.
Come by the store around 11 alright?

INT. Day. The Sev.

Sandy Sev hands Jonny a package. [of what?]

JONNY

Sandy Sev is my supplier. She doesn't deal
directly anymore because it's become a bit of a big
business. Besides, she volunteers at the drop-in centre
and she wants to focus on helping at-risk youth.

[seems like a contradiction]

INT. Day. Drop-in centre. Sandy has her arms around the
skater kids. And they are all smiling wide, exaggerated

"happy family" smiles. [handwritten: why?]

INT. Day. Shill Station. Jonny is behind the counter. He looks at the reader and rolls his eyes. [handwritten: why eye roll?]

INT. Night. Back of the Shill Station. By lamplight, Jonny is cutting the cocaine with baby formula. [handwritten: i don't follow.]

JONNY

I know Sandy Sev used to cut her coke with baby formula too. One of the tricks of the trade. It's kind of necessary if you want to make a profit. And besides, there's nothing unhealthy about baby formula. I'm giving these kids some much-needed vitamins and nutrients.

EXT. Night. The two skater kids are peering in the window and they see Jonny mixing the coke and formula, dispensing it into little dime bags.

EXT. Night, Shill parking lot. Jonny meets the skater kids by his Chevette.

JONNY

Hey Guys! Ready to hit the slopes? [handwritten: ski Trip not established!]

SKATER KID #2

Oh yeah, Jonny. We're fucking ready. [handwritten: vulgar. unnecessar]

SKATER KID #1

Hit the slopes? How about you hit the cement! *as in skateboard?*

Skater Kid #1 lifts his board over his head and slams it over Jonny's face. Both kids give Jonny the beats until he is left in a bruised, bloody heap. *oh my!*

EXT. Shill parking lot. Morning. Jonny lies next to his Chevette in the fetal position as the sun rises. Dora rushes over to him and cradles him. *nicely done!*

DORA

Jonny! Who did this to you?

Jonny squints at Dora.

JONNY

The kids. I tried to rip them off. I deserved it.

DORA

Jesus Christ. Your lip is split. You need stitches.

avoid using the Lord's name in vain.

JONNY

No. No doctors. I'm already feeling better. Please?

Dora picks up Jonny and helps him walk.

INT. Day. Dora's apartment. Dora pours solvent on Jonny's face, gives him a swig of Jameson, and stitches up Jonny's lip.

[handwritten: ↖ the solvent??]

DORA

All these years of sewing at Libby's Discount Fabrics finally pay off.

JONNY (as Dora pokes the needle through)

Fuck! Fucking hell! *[handwritten: || vulgar!]*

DORA

You're living with me from now on.
Fuck this parking lot bullshit. *[handwritten: enough!]*

JONNY

Really? Thanks, Dora.

DORA

Whatever.

EXT. Day. Strip mall parking lot. *[handwritten: what frame?]*

Dora stands outside of the frame, left. Larger than life. Breaks the fourth wall, addresses the reader.

[handwritten: what does this mean?   Sigh...]

148

DORA

Okay. Listen. Jonny's never going to get this right.

This is what happened to our strip mall . . .

confusing.

INT. Day. Libby's Discount Fabrics.

Two bald, fifty-something men in dark suits are talking to
Libby (an elderly spinster-looking woman)

DORA (Narrating)

The Hypermart lawyers and agents moved quickly.

They provided some pretty big incentives for
store owners to break their leases.

like what

literally or figuratively?

INT. Day. Blip's Arcade.

The two men in dark suits talking to Blip. Blip shakes one
of their hands. And looks very pleased.

who is this now??

DORA

Some people were more than happy to get
a little extra cash to bail on the strip mall. Some
businesses were not built to last.

this is how the free market works!

INT. Day. Drop-in centre

Sandy Sev crosses her arms and looks indignantly at the
two men.

why?

DORA

Other places were not businesses at all.

But it's easy to pay off the city…

INT. Night. Libby's Discount Fabrics.

Libby is signing papers while the two men smugly look on.

what do the papers say?

DORA

Eventually we all fell. Except the two corporate entities:

the Shill Station and the Sev. But all the mom-and-pop

shops closed. Even Libby. She was the last to go.

is this an anti-corporate story?

EXT. Day. Strip mall overhead.

Construction site. The stores are demolished, leaving only

rubble, the Shill, and the Sev. (Two panels.) Then the

Hypermart is erected. Two panels: construction and

completion.

so

Dora out of frame below fourth panel, hands on hips, looks

up at the completed Hypermart.

confusing!

DORA

And there she is: Hypermart Store 157.

And as for us, there was some promise for our future. We

were all considered prospective Hypermart associates.

great!

INT. Day. Hypermart.

The grand opening of Hypermart Store 157. Balloons, ribbons, streamers, banners. Dora, Libby, Blip, Henry . . . all wearing blue smocks (grey . . .) waving and smiling at the reader as if the reader is the customer. *How nice!*

INT. Day. Hypermart. Jonny wanders the aisles aimlessly in an unbuttoned smock and untucked shirt. *|(not professional*

DORA

Eventually even Jonny joined the Hypermart family.

INT. Day. Hypermart. Dora is putting stock on the shelves. (Housewares — so maybe linens?) *don't ask, tell. and don't tell, show!*

DORA

It wasn't a very happy family. It was a minimum wage, unpaid overtime, no future, "open door policy" family. All we had to do was "buy in." We couldn't afford not to. But *double negative* as a result we could afford very little in our own lives. Most

of us were living paycheque to paycheque.

INT. Day. Hypermart staff room.

she's a judge??

Libby is holding court. Other associates are huddled around her.

DORA

Libby even tried to get us organized.
There were unions we could join. In fact, there was
a large union who was trying to bring Hypermart
employees into the fold and challenge. This was, after all,
Transcona. A labour town. We could do something
to help ourselves and our comrades.

this sounds communist!!

INT. Night. Hypermart manager's office. Libby is sitting at
the desk. Hardman and Linville are red-faced. They are
pointing and yelling at her. Libby is wide-eyed and
horrified. *good!*

DORA *no!*

I'm not sure what those fuckers said to Libby,
but she didn't stick around.

INT. Day. A recently cleared lot is now a construction
site. *|| already done*

DORA

Then, after a few years, the Hypermart corporation
did something strange. They purchased more retail space
only five kilometres away from Store 157, on the west side
of Transcona, and within months, they erected

Store 178. A Hypermart megastore.
This makes no sense.

EXT. Day. Hypermart 178 parking lot. Store 178 grand opening.

what does smock mean?

Dora, wearing a Hypermart smock, hands in pockets, outside the frame.

DORA

Some of the more diligent employees were
offered transfers to the new megastore. They offered
me as close to full time as possible without having to pay
me any benefits. They offered Jonny nothing. But we were
ready to move to Montreal for grad school, armed
with student loans. It was a real fucking pleasure
to turn them down.

as they should be!

enough! swearing is not helping.

INT. Day. Hardman's office. Dora gives Hardman the finger. Hardman doesn't seem to care.

—> why? your story needs to be nicer.

EXT. Night. An empty Hypermart. No signage. Completely closed down. The Sev boarded up, the Shill Station remains.

I didn't guess!

lots of fragments.

DORA

As you have may have guessed, Store 157 didn't last
another fiscal year. Hypermart left an empty
box-shaped tomb in our old strip mall and East Transcona
was a ghost town.

literally OR figuratively?

153

EXT. Day. Empty strip mall parking lot. Jonny and Dora are holding hands and walking away *from each other?? while holding hands??*

DORA

Jonny and I were on to bigger and better things. I had been accepted to Montreal University for Doctoral Studies in Developmental Psychology. And Jonny was growing more confident by the day. He knew that he was going to be a writer. A good one. And I was more than willing to help him. I believed in Jonny.

This ending falls flat.

Jonny,
Thanks for sharing your writing. The stuff you think of in your brain! OH BOY! You are a real nut! (in a good way!) Now, I have to tell you that this isn't the kind of movie/comic book/or play or whatever that I would take Sarah and the kids to, or buy for them, whatever the case may be, but I can tell you worked very hard, and there's not a lot of spelling mistakes, so BRAVO!
Stan Steinberg

Initial Stripmalling Sketches

BY EVAN

157

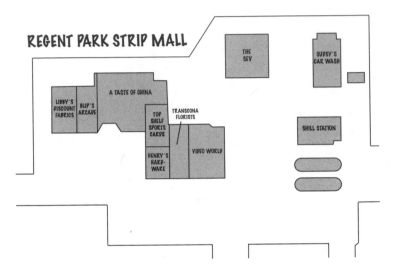

REGENT PARK STRIP MALL

THE SEV

SUDSY'S CAR WASH

LIBBY'S DISCOUNT FABRICS

BLIP'S ARCADE

A TASTE OF CHINA

TOP SHELF SPORTS CARDS

TRANSCONA FLORISTS

HENRY'S HARDWARE

VIDEO WORLD

SHILL STATION

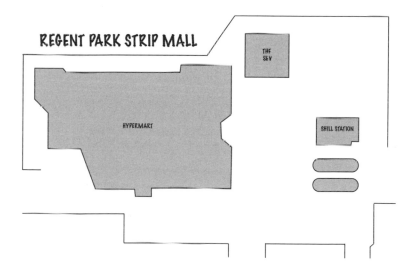

REGENT PARK STRIP MALL

THE
SEV

HYPERMART

SHILL STATION

Final Credits:
Lame Teen Comedy
Freeze Frame Wrapups

Jonny continues to live alone in Montreal, where he works as a part-time university instructor, a C-level comedy writer, and a poet. He sells drugs to his students to supplement his income.

Dora quit her job as a tenured professor of developmental psychology to become a rocket scientist.

Evan left Montreal for Toronto where he is a successful male escort, and, in his spare time, designs and produces edible erotic underpants.

Sandy Sev is a minister at the United Church of Transcona.

Carmen Adams died. Remember? It was very sad.

Skater Kid #1 was the valedictorian of his graduating class.

Skater Kid #2 is studying to be a social worker.

Mr. Stubler is still the proud owner of a Shill station.

Jonny's parents still worship Jesus Christ.

Jonny's brother still worships Satan.

Hypermart continues to ruin towns across North America.

Stripmalling became a book and you just finished reading it. Its critical and commercial fate is yet to be determined, but it's not looking good.

Acknowledgements

Thanks to my amazing daughter, Lilly Fiorentino, and all of my family for their endless support and love.

Thanks to Marisa Grizenko.

Thanks to Tara Flanagan, Ian Orti, Darren Bifford, Sophie Caird, Mike Spry, David McGimpsey, derek beaulieu, Jason Camlot, Mikhail Iossel, Jeff Parker (and everyone at SLS St. Petersburg), Karin Zuppiger, Melissa Bull, Sarah Steinberg, Anne Stone, Sachiko Murakami, Jessica Johnson, Andy Brown, Zoe Whittall, Alana Wilcox, MC Palassio, Darren Wershler, Jason Christie, Jason Camlot, and Craig Silverman.

Thanks to early editors of this text: Stuart Ross, Maria Erskine, Elizabeth Koch, Jeremy Leipert, Dimitri Katadotis, Brian Kaufman, Maya Merrick, and Elizabeth Bachinsky.

Special thanks to the Canada Council for the Arts for supporting me through the writing of this book.

Very special thanks to Evan Munday, a great partner in crime and a dear friend.

Very special thanks to Jennifer Knoch for her amazing proofreading.

Very special thanks to Rachel Ironstone for her awesome design work.

Very special thanks to my editor, Michael Holmes, for his support over the years and sharing a vision.

Publication Notes

Parts of this novel have appeared on CBC Radio One's *All in a Weekend,* and in *THIS Magazine, filling Station, Word, Event, Matrix, sub-Terrain,* and *Opium.*

Other Titles by Jon Paul Fiorentino